KATE

KATE

CHET KINSEY

CUTTING EDGE

ISBN-13: 978-1-962896-97-9

Published by
Cutting Edge Books
PO Box 8212
Calabasas, CA 91372
www.cuttingedgebooks.com

CHAPTER ONE

F ASCINATED, Kate Flick stared at the five ten-dollar bills, straight from the purity of the mint. They were so clean, so crisp, so beautiful and absorbing, like new keys to unlock the gate of a world she had never known. For a long moment, she forgot the unctuous man who sat behind the wheel of the coupe.

"I'm going to be rich, rich, rich!" Kate murmured. The words lilted off her lips, an iteration of exultation and expectancy. "Yes, rich, rich!"

The coupe stood parked under a leafing maple on a narrow sidestreet in Newark, New Jersey. A row of houses, lining the street, leaned against one another like ugly, patient old men.

Ray Ungas stared at Kate, one hand nonchalant on the wheel, the fingernails tinged with black dirt. He was a small, thin man, twenty-eight years old, with the toughness of the back alleys showing in his face.

"Kid," Ray offered expansively, "you're gonna be rich an' famous." His left eyebrow cocked, posing a question. "When's your birthday?"

Smiling, Kate turned to face Ray. "Don't you remember?" She pouted prettily. "I've dreamed and dreamed of tomorrow! I'll be seventeen!"

Ray uncocked the eyebrow nervously. "Damn," he swore under his breath. "Look, I thought you said eighteen your next birthday."

"No, when we first met in February—" Some unpleasant recollection blotted out the elation on Kate's young face. "Sixteen and never been kissed, I told you that—that first time."

Ray's fingers tightened on the wheel. "Kid, you got a birth certificate around?"

"Ummm, I don't think Dad has one."

Her hair was a warm, soft brown, the natural curl hidden by a silly hat, maroon-and-white, the colors of Newark's Eastern High School. Her eyes were large, and the irises had the velvety, incredible wetness of violet pansies.

Kate wondered: "What about my birth certificate?"

"It don't matter."

"Why did you ask?"

"I said it don't matter! Ray flounced around on the worn cushion. "Just be sure you look more'n seventeen years old when we go up to Westchester. Pass off for nineteen—maybe twenty-one."

"But I don't want to be twenty-one, yet!" Kate protested, and made a face. "Why twenty-one—that's positively ancient! Why should I be like twenty-one?"

"For him."

Kate's lips parted. She leaned close to Ray. "Danny," she asked breathlessly, "wants me to look like an—an old woman of twenty-one?"

"Sure, Danny Dorman, my old pal in grade school." Ray's dark eyes were hungry, but Kate didn't notice. "Danny Dorman—" Ray's lips patted the name—"him that's got his own TV show now. And once, I thought he hadda voice like a girl!"

"In church, Danny was a boy soprano!" Kate said rapturously. "He's a baritone today and—oh, he sends me!" She shivered deliciously.

"Get real," Ray said, and patted Kate's hand that clasped the five ten-dollar bills. "Tomorrow, you got a birthday an' you're only seventeen. A minor still, see?" Kate nodded. "Now, tomorrow you start the new, grand life. Today, it don't make a difference if you're seventeen, but where you're going you better be—uh, we make the age twenty."

"For Danny?"

"Sure."

"Danny wants me to—to act like twenty!"

"Sure."

"I'll act like twenty years old for Danny! I like to act. In my own room at home, I'm always acting. I'm a model or maybe a blues singer like—"

"Look," Ray interrupted impatiently, "stop dreaming, kid. That fifty dollars is yours every week—if you're smart and listen to me—from our mutual friend, Danny Dorman. We work the pitch together, see? You do like I say."

Kate's smooth brow furrowed. "Pitch?"

"This is—well, like a game."

"Ray—"

Kate's voice acquired a tremulous, childish overtone.

"It's not wrong to take this money, is it? I mean, Danny does want me to have it! That's not bad, is it?"

"What's bad, huh?" Ray grinned loosely. "Nothing's bad if you think it's good. Now, nobody has to know you got that money, see? If you don't get caught with the money, it's all right."

"Caught?"

"Well, if your parents found that money on you—that's what *caught* is." Ray wet his lips. "Your old man'd whip the tar outa you. See what I mean?"

Kate shuddered, remembering the time father had whipped her with a belt because she was wearing lipstick. Her fingers tightened and she became aware of the crisp bills again.

So beautiful, all that money! More than she had ever seen before. Well, the most she had ever seen in her own hands!

"Ray." Kate's voice was a strained whisper. "I want to feel clean, absolutely clean about this money." Her voice turned fierce. "Since I met you—that first night at your rooms—Ray, I've taken a hot bath every day! I've scrubbed and soaped my body because I want to be clean, always! I can't stand things that are dirty!" She shivered against the cushions, putting space between them. "Those pretty clothes you bought for me—that's why I let you—" Kate stopped. "Ray, we've been clean together! No secrets—except our meetings! It's—it's all right to keep this money?"

"Sure, Danny wanted you to have it. Don't worry, kid. In this, we're both clean!"

If there were a difference in the way he had said the word, Kate missed the inflection. For the moment, she was satisfied.

"Fifty dollars every week, all my own!" she breathed. "And I'll work hard where I'm going, do whatever Danny wants me to do!" She stared at the money. "But I don't want to do anything bad, Ray. And we weren't bad together! Not those four times! You've been good to me and—Danny wants me to keep the money?"

"Sure," Ray said. "I'll tuck it in the bank."

Folding the bills twice over, he tucked them into the bank of her white, ribbed sock. "There, all yours."

"Why did Danny want me to have the money, Ray?"

"Maybe he plans to put you in his show—uh, later."

"Really?"

"Sure, Danny likes you."

"And that's all of it?"

"The rest is like a game. Danny lost."

"How did Danny lose, Ray?"

Ray shrugged. "It's like a game of craps. If you lose, you gotta pay up. That's the rules, see? Don't worry, every week Danny wants to pay you."

"Does Danny pay you?"

"Me?" Ray laughed. "Unh, unh."

"Can't you tell me more about this game?" Kate pleaded.

"Maybe. In a big city, kid, you gotta think of number one or you're a sap." Ray explained glibly. "Danny's no sap so he hit the big-time. Nobody gives a sap a break. Saps get stepped on, like ants. I know. I was a sap. This is a democracy, right?" Ray paused and Kate nodded. "Well, in a democracy, everybody is equal. Yeah? Look at Danny Dorman an' me. We went to the same school, played on the same block, kissed the same girls, and stole from the five-and-dime together. So, we got older an' we don't steal no more. Stealing's wrong, kid. Now, Danny an' I was pals. Danny gets the break with that voice and I drive a delivery truck."

Ray's eyes widened and his fingers gripped the wheel.

"Man, Danny hauls down over a quarter-million every year and can't even spend all the money the government don't grab! But Danny's got a heart, kid. He remembered Ray Ungas. Danny met you through me. So, Danny gave this money to me—for you. He don't miss it. It's yours an' there's more where this came from."

"I'd do anything for Danny Dorman," Kate said proudly, her eyes shining. "I was president of the North Street Danny Dorman Fan Club! Yes, I'd do anything for Danny!"

"Sure you would. In fact, kid, you did."

"Ray, I explained that! It was just—"

"Never mind explaining again," Ray interrupted. "I'll tell you a bit more about this—uh, this game. Sometimes, I don't understand you, kid. You want to come up to my place an' you don't want to come. Only four times you come an' I wanted it to be a hundred! Well, that night in late March, when you sneaked outa your old man's house an' came up there—I knew you was waiting, but I had a date with Danny. I said to Danny, 'Let's have a drink,' an' I bought him a drink. Danny bought some more rounds an' I said, 'Let's go up to my rooms and get bombed.' You know, like old times, kid."

Intent, Kate listened, but Ray seemed to drift off as he continued to talk.

"So, we come up to the place. You was scared an' hid in the closet, not knowin' it was Danny Dorman. Me an' Danny killed a bottle. I knew you wanted to meet Danny, bein' in his fan club an' all. Danny's a great guy. So, I opened the closet an' you tumbled out. Right off, Danny seen you was something special. You are one beautiful babe, kid. Damn, he seen you in makeup and that nightgown I bought for nine bucks and—well, you two got along swell, you sittin' on Danny's lap an' that nightgown so thin—"

Ray's thin face darkened.

"You didn't mind when Danny sent me out for more liquor. I come back an' you an' Danny were on the bed an'—"

"Ray! He asked me to!"

"Look, I don't blame Danny. Danny had too many drinks an' you're a beautiful babe an' Danny don't know you're only—jeez, you looked like twenty years old that night, kid!"

She was upset by the retelling of that tale, tried to avoid listening to what Ray was saying. "Ray," she gasped, "I couldn't say no! I—I love Danny!"

"You didn't have to love him that much." Ray grinned. "Forget about it, kid. Danny's my pal."

She couldn't forget it, kept going over it. The way Danny had looked, just like on TV and she had seen him next door on the Mayberry's twenty-one-inch screen. The blond curl that always dangled over his forehead … the deep blue of his eyes … the half-twist to his lips … the way he had held her close and … Ray had come back!

Kate said suddenly: "Ray, what did Danny do with the picture you took?"

"Kept it."

"Danny has it now?"

"Sure, keeps it in his wallet. Makes me jealous, kid. You with no gown on and—"

"Ray, please!"

"Okay." Ray shrugged. "Danny'd see you more, but he's got a wife who's a crank an' two kids. Danny remembers you all the time. That's why he sent the money. Kid, there's only one thing I don't like about this." Ray moved closer. "Since that night with Danny, you haven't been to my place, not once. What's come over you, huh?"

"Ray, I've been busy."

"Okay, you've been busy. But Danny still remembers you. Danny will always remember you, believe me. That's why he sent that fifty bucks. Danny said, 'Buy Kate nylons an' stuff.' With this money, kid, you can go places, buy what you need. You look like a jerk in those cheap duds your old man makes you wear. Look at yourself, now! Think Danny Dorman'd look twice at you?"

The dinky maroon hat had a white button on the top. She wore a sloppy sweatshirt covered with the careless scrawls of other kids, and the biggest legend said: DANNY DORMAN FAN CLUB. The skirt was a cheap plaid—too full, too long, too old, with a darned tear at one thigh. The ribbed socks had loose tops from too many launderings, but everything she wore was scrupulously clean, even the old saddle-shoes, clean.

"—your eyes," Ray was saying. "I spotted 'em first. Bedroom eyes I tole myself an' got interested. Like I tole you outside the candy store, you was made for nylons an' mink, not kid duds. An' you thought I was on the make, didn't you? Not Ray Ungas! I wanted to have you look decent in some real clothes an' you come up to my house an' found out I was your friend. Well, tomorrow you're eigh—uh, seventeen an' a big girl. You should be on your own. I know this place up in Westchester an' Danny wants you to go there an'—"

His hand fumbled at the hem of the cheap plaid skirt. When he caressed her smooth, young thigh, Kate shivered and broke out in gooseflesh. The hand was hot, sweaty and insistent. Its clamminess repelled her. She captured the hand and held it tight with all her young strength.

"Ray—please!" She tried to coax a promise into her voice. "Wait until—later!" Her voice was a choked sound.

"Okay," Ray grumbled, "I'll settle for a kiss."

"Not here, someone might see!"

"Look, I'll park further down the street tonight, say ten o'clock." Ray eyed her sharply. "When will you go up to Westchester to that place, huh?"

"I—I don't know!"

"Meet me tonight?"

"Ray, it's so hard to get out!"

"I'll wait an'—"

Kate slid from the coupe. "Bye," she said.

"Look, ten o'clock if you can get out an'—"

Kate hurried off. Behind her, she heard the engine of Ray's car start up, then the coupe gunned off with a shrill shriek of tires on asphalt, Ray's flamboyant method of driving.

Ray Ungas, Kate thought bitterly. I—I hate him. After Danny Dorman—

She shivered deliciously.

She turned a corner, hurried down another block, passed quickly by the familiar candy store, and entered North Street Three teenage would-be hoods stood there, hands in pockets of blue jeans with wide belts studded with brass, cigarettes limp in slack lips, and shoulders supporting the big glass window of the candy store. One yawned around a cigarette and another one said casually: "Hiya, kid."

Kate said, "Hi," and hurried past.

Behind her, someone groaned: "What a hunk of lard."

"Maybe with the clothes off she—"

"Nuts, too fat."

Kate blushed. *You're lovely,* she had heard Danny Dorman say.

Yes, lovely!

It was these horrid clothes she was forced to wear, and the lack of makeup because her father insisted cosmetics were cheap. Well, Kate thought, If I walked past those three fools at the corner in that black nightgown hidden at home, their eyes would pop and—

What did they matter? They were squares.

Danny Dorman mattered, but not Ray. Ray was an old man.

Oh, if Danny weren't married! And wasn't it nice of Danny to remember her and send money for better clothes and—

How, she wondered, would she ever be able to buy and wear decent clothes? And she certainly would need nice things if she ever got to that place in Westchester. What kind of place was it? Not a dump like this!

North Street was shabbily sedate. Kate climbed a short flight of stone steps to the starved level of lawn, remembering that since arthritis had crippled her father things at home had gone from bad to worse.

She stopped suddenly and stared. There in the corner by the steps, a golden daffodil bloomed, bloomed in this, the first week of May. Last fall she had bought a single daffodil bulb for a nickel in the five-and-dime and had planted it in this corner of the yard because the sunlight could reach it there. She remembered the name: *Magnificence.* And it had bloomed gloriously, just as the picture had advertised—a huge, glowing, golden thing of beauty. And all hers!

If I had money, Kate thought, I'd buy a thousand flowers just like that lonely one!

Magnificence! Such a rich, regal sound to the name.

Fifty dollars in her sock!

Hundreds of golden daffodils in her sock!

Gaily, she danced up the creaky steps and reached for the door handle. Her eyes hardened. There were two signs by the bell. The one above the bell read: LEROY M. FLICK. The one below the bell said more primly: ERNESTINE BALLANTINE and TERESE ROWE. The two old maids who had rented the upstairs!

When her father first hung that FOR RENT sign in the front window, Kate recalled bitterly, she had taken it down, fearing that if the upstairs were rented she would lose her pretty bedroom and be forced to sleep downstairs in the—well, it hadn't been the dining room! Her parents had claimed that room for their own and had let the entire second floor to those perfectly horrid old maids. Now Kate slept in the pantry.

A birthday tomorrow. Seventeen and her own boss. I'll throw the old maids out, she thought, and move back into the sunny bedroom I had before.

She opened the door quietly and sniffed. Oh, God! Cabbage again tonight!

Cabbage was cheap, full of vitamins. And the short, string end of a ham was cheap too. What was life here? Cabbage and ham, and not very much ham at that.

CHAPTER TWO

DARKNESS filled the alleys between the close-set houses on North Street. Kate had washed the supper dishes, scrubbed the chipped sink, swept the kitchen floor, and rinsed out some underwear.

From the direction of the dining room, her father's voice drifted faintly into the kitchen. When he said heavily, "Amen," her mother echoed ratification of the Biblical passage. Then her father began to read another chapter.

Night and day, always the Bible reading, Kate thought, gesturing helplessly. Not that she didn't appreciate the Bible. But if there were only less Bible in this house, more love and freedom! Yes, and more money.

This "place" in Westchester that Ray Ungas always talked about—what was it like?

Westchester, Ray had said, offered escape from this prison of a home. A promise of freedom and more. It would be—yes, on the drive to Westchester, an opportunity for Ray to park the coupe and pet. And petting would lead to more than kissing.

I can't stand his clammy hands, Kate thought, remembering that first night she had gone to Ray's flat.

When her parents had been sound asleep, she had slipped from this house, and had practically run the six blocks. Then she had been all a-tremble, inexperienced with a man, not knowing what was going to happen next.

Ray had been unhurried. "Look," he had reasoned, "it's all right for you to come to a decent place. Gets you free from those nutsy parents. Now, those kid duds you wear are all wrong for a gorgeous figure like yours. So, I shelled out some money and bought you something special, kid."

Ray had brought out a black bra-panty set in nylon and a pair of gorgeous stockings. "Bet you never owned anything like these," Ray had gloated. "Look, you got the build of a woman. Go in the bedroom, try these on. And close the door tight. I promise not to peek. And take a good, long look at yourself in the mirror and see how you like the presents."

For a moment, Kate had stood in the bedroom, wondering if it were wrong to be there, if she dared try on the presents. The lacy lingerie was so tempting. She couldn't resist the lovely things which had always been denied her and soon forgot about right and wrong in her hurried effort to strip off the awkward kid clothes. Firm, young breasts had thrust forward to fill the bra and long, curved legs had slid into the panties. Pulling them on her hips, she had turned.

There in the mirror! Such a curvesome study of white flesh and black nylon like—she had laughed happily—like a panda!

Her hair had been all wrong and she had used a military brush to sweep the brown masses higher and pin them fast. She had been so engrossed she had not heard the door open and Ray enter until he had said: "Kid, you look like a million bucks!"

Terrified by his entrance, Kate had wheeled. "Ray! You promised not to—"

"Jeez, you really fill that stuff out!" Kate had liked the compliment. "All yours for one kiss, okay?"

She hadn't wanted him to touch her but, she had foolishly reasoned, what was one kiss in payment for the lovely things he had bought her?

Inevitably, one kiss had led to many. Kate had been overwhelmed by the caresses, the murmuring, the heavenly compliments. At first, she had been timid, then some strange, inexplicable emotion had erupted like fireworks through her body and she had kissed Ray wildly, scarcely aware of what his quick, moist hands were doing to her virginal body.

On the bed, she had sobbed: "You—we mustn't!"

"I'll be careful."

She was sixteen years old, but she had known it was wrong. There had been the hurting rudeness at first, then the relaxation under his coachings, and finally the inexplicable surging upward with all her body under the spell of some inner madness.

Afterward, she had been ashamed, vowing never to sneak to his rooms again, but there had been the lure of a new dress, perfume, a shiny hand-mirror, high-heeled white opera pumps, a sheer nightgown, things that she had often seen in shop windows, had admired and craved, but things far beyond the Flick pocketbook. To yield her body to him for a few moments had seemed inconsequential, and twice more she had visited his rooms.

But the night that Danny Dorman had come unexpectedly and she had tumbled from the closet as Ray had opened the door—that had been so, so important! Ray Ungas was repulsive, his hands calloused, the nails broken and filthy. But Danny was—oh, so heavenly!

How she had trembled under his first kiss, she remembered. And what a dreamy madness there had been in her strugglings on the bed. Then that fool Ray had blundered into the room. How she detested Ray.

Why had Ray fetched out the camera and taken a photograph of her in Danny's strong arms? Danny giggling drunkenly, and not a stitch on her!

Standing alone in this bleak, dreary kitchen, Kate Flick flushed fiery red.

Must it end with that one, wonderful time? Never no more, Danny Dorman? Would she never see him again?

Smiling to herself, Kate stepped into the pantry-bedroom and closed the door. She tugged on a pull-cord.

Overhead, a forty-watt bulb glowed eerily and she saw the horribly cracked ceiling and the dingy walls that a scrubbrush had failed to clean. The room was tinily square, barely enough space for a cot and pine bureau, but she did not feel cramped.

A kewpie doll stood atop the bureau, a school pennant hung limply on one wall, and some thumbed books lined one of the shelves. Kate liked one book best, "Stars To Steer By," a wonderful title for an anthology of poems. In this quiet silence, she sat on the cot under the glaring bulb and read the poems that let her drift into the dream-world of the poets.

She felt fully self-possessed and adult in this pantry-room. Her parents never came in here. And it wasn't a pantry, really, but a room in a palace, where fresh dreams burgeoned forth.

Shielding the lower shelves was a cretonne curtain and behind the curtain many empty, dusty Mason jars, rusted iron pots and dented pans, odds and ends discarded long ago, including a roasting pan that had stood neglected. This pan used to hold a turkey on every holiday. How long had it been since this house had known a roasted turkey? Four— no, five years! And the pan was too large to hold a scrawny chicken.

Most important of all in this room was the secret behind two tall canisters. The cylinders hid a battered handbag, which contained the new clothes Ray Ungas had purchased for the "trip to Westchester."

Westchester seemed miles and miles away, like Chicago, because Kate had never traveled. Must I leave this room, Kate wondered, for the unknown?

Yet, the hidden handbag tempted her with the rare promise of more lovely clothes. So did the fifty-dollars in her sock, dollars she dared not spend if she stayed here. Suddenly, she knew she could not go away with Ray Ungas. With Danny Dorman—yes! She wanted nothing more to do with Ray. The fifty-dollars every week wasn't from Ray really, but a present from Danny who wanted her to become rich and famous.

Tomorrow, Kate decided, I'll tell Ray I want to finish my last year in high school. In June—or never—I'll go to Westchester. She thought more deeply. Ray thought I would be eighteen, not seventeen, tomorrow. I'm still a minor. Does that worry him? If I get in trouble, they'll print his name in the newspaper, but not mine.

Trouble?

Ray had said, "I'll be careful," but Danny hadn't been careful. Still, there was a way of knowing there was no trouble. Last week her time had come and passed.

So, in her mind, the familiar was reassuring; the unknown somewhat puzzling and frightening, like being on a strange airplane and the pilot not knowing where he was going.

As she draped the sweatshirt over the bureau, she patted the name in the legend, DANNY DORMAN FAN CLUB. Dear Danny, so sweet! And when he sang, a voice just like—like rain on velvet. Kate wriggled from the skirt and petticoat, set the saddle shoes under the cot, pulled off one sock. The beautiful, new bills that Danny had sent dropped out.

In this room, the bills were just as lovely as they had been in Ray's coupe.

Good heavens, there was no hurry to leave tonight or any night for Westchester!

By the end of June at fifty dollars a week, she calculated, I'll have over three hundred dollars. Enough money to make my way anywhere alone and no need for that horrid Ray Ungas. I'll be able to get along without him.

Kate hid the bills in the tip of one shoe. There, out of sight from her parents' prying eyes, the bills were safe. But then, her parents never came into the pantry, anyway.

Now that the decision had been made to stay here for several months, Kate relaxed. She hummed a snatch of song and unhooked the worn bra and stood in pink scanties. From the bureau, she brought out the shiny new hand-mirror Ray had given her, fluffed her hair idly and admired her reflection.

Ummm, she decided, the eyes are best. Deep and soft and limpid, almost violet in color. And what had Ray meant by saying, "You have bedroom eyes?" Weren't all eyes bedroom eyes—in a bedroom?

She liked the fullness of her lips, particularly half-parted on the verge of a smile, and the white, even teeth. Her skin glowed, smooth and clean from much soaping. The breasts were firm, ripe mounds and rather high on her chest, but were rudely ridged from the constrictiveness of the worn bra. Delicate fingers rubbed out the ridges. Under the pressuring, the points hardened inexplicably. That had happened before—with Ray, then with Danny. Again, a delicious emotion stirred inside her body, seeming to center—no, flow into the nipples.

"Danny said you were beautiful," she murmured rapturously. "So beautiful in nakedness."

Inhaling, Kate swelled the chest cavity, quarter-turned to the hand mirror, a trick she had learned from reading a magazine article. Under the rib cage, the stomach that had never known the confinement of a disciplining girdle flattened into nothing. Kate stretched lazily, one arm lifted to the ceiling. Rising on tiptoes, she yawned and stretched. There was cat-like grace in every fluent movement of head and arm and chest, and every curve was a youthful promise.

"So lovely, lovely," Kate murmured rapturously. "Without any clothes, so undreamed of, lovely and—"

At her back, the door opened.

Kate wheeled, startled by the interruption.

Gaunt and glowering, father stood in the doorway, lips a stern line above a chin shadowed with unshaved beard. Behind him, staring in, Kate saw her mother's graying hair and doughy face and fat body.

Covering her breasts, Kate shrank back aghast. "You've no right!" she gasped. "You—you should have knocked!"

"This is my house," father said heavily. "Where did you get that mirror?"

You're caught! Kate thought wildly, struggling to control the emotion that turned her muscles into gelatine. How did they know about the mirror? Who spied in here? If they knew about Ray or found out about him—never mind Ray! They must never find out about Danny Dorman!

Turning, Kate jerked a light coat from a wall hook. Fumbling fingers held the garment between her nudity and her parents.

Father mumbled, "Praise God, she's a woman grown," as if he had discovered the secret of the universe.

"Didn't I tell you so?" mother snapped. "Didn't I tell you she's chesty as a woman? Where'd she get that mirror, Leroy? It must have cost five dollars, Leroy. Now, where'd she get five dollars to buy that mirror, Leroy?" With an elbow, mother pressed father's back. "Don't stand there, Leroy. I told you she had a mirror hidden in here. What are you going to do about the mirror, Leroy? Are you going to stand there shiftless while vanity poisons God's house, Leroy?"

The father stood hesitant.

Kate cried out: "You've no right to burst in here! With me like this, you can't!"

"I didn't realize," father groaned. "A woman grown."

"And staring at her sinful nakedness in that mirror," her mother rasped. "What are you going to do to her, Leroy?"

The father seemed to awaken. He reached out and tore the coat from Kate's hands. "Woman," he demanded, "where did you get that sinful mirror?"

Kate shrank back and pressed her body into the narrow space between wall and bureau.

Father said: "Who is he, woman?"

"He?" Kate stammered.

"Mirrors don't grow on trees. What did you do for him that he gave you money to buy a mirror?"

Kate began to get a firm grip on her fears. He and him, father had said, as if he meant some stranger. They didn't know, couldn't know about Danny Dorman. The fools! They didn't even suspect a Ray Ungas.

"There is no he," Kate said.

"Smiling at us and staring at your woman-nakedness in that sinful mirror! God, damn her soul! How long has he been after you and you naked with him, young slut?"

Blood drained from Kate's face. "I'm no slut," she flared. "There is no man."

"Told you she wasn't a child," the mother cackled. "Told you, when I found that mirror, that there had to be a man."

"You lie!" Kate said, hating her mother.

"Breasts of a woman grown, white as a dove," the father said. "Oh, Lord, why hast thou visited more misery unto my humble household?" He brushed one hand awkwardly across his face, his movements those of a man crippled from arthritis. "Woman, is there more of vanity in this room?"

If they searched, Kate realized, they would find the telltale handbag.

"Only the mirror," she whimpered, resorting to a trick of cringing she had learned as a child.

"Where did the mirror come from, woman?"

Kate said the first thing that popped into her head. "I—I found it!"

"Where?"

"In the park."

"What park?"

"Branch Brook!"

"Were you to the park with a man, woman?"

"No!"

"What else did you find in the park?"

"Only the mirror. Someone must have—well, lost it. Please, leave me alone!"

The father might have left, but not the mother. She hissed, "We are God-like people, Leroy, and you must punish her." Saliva drooled from the corners of her mother's mouth. "When will you punish her for her wickedness, Leroy?"

Father picked up the mirror.

"Vanity, all is vanity in this room," her father intoned, and a paroxysm of anger shivered through his thin shoulders. "Vanity, the devil's curse!" He hurled the mirror against one sidewall. The glass shattered and spewed shards around the tiny pantry. "The end of the devil's vanity!"

They will go now, Kate thought hopefully.

"What about her, Leroy?" mother said.

For the first time, Kate saw her mother clearly. Always, when she had been punished by her father, she had blamed him. Now, she saw the cruel, inner temper of her mother and knew that time after time it had been this vicious woman who had spurred her father into punishment. And no wonder! Fat and dumpy, ugly and sullen, the mother hated the beautiful daughter.

"Did she find that mirror in the park, Leroy?" the mother demanded. "Hah, I've heard tales of what loose women and girls do in Branch Brook Park, Leroy! Men fumble under their clothes—and do more than that. And not one man with her, Leroy. Many men, Leroy. Any man, Leroy." There seemed no depth to the woman's viciousness. "So, she went to the park? And not to find any mirror, Leroy."

The mother talked, Kate realized, with the same intensity that possessed her as she listened to the endless reading of Scriptures. Was this woman sane?

"—and my house, Leroy, is become a house of shame because of her. She will drive God from our house, Leroy, and we will be friendless. Do you want God driven from our house, Leroy? She fetched the devil in here, she gave herself to men, and—"

"You lie!" Kate cried out.

"Leroy! Will you stand there and let that whore call your true wife vile names?"

Father shivered, closed his eyes. His fingers worked convulsively, but still he hesitated.

The mother thrust a leather strap into his hand. "Scourge her, Leroy," she urged. "Scourge sin and Satan from her naked body, Leroy."

The father opened his eyes. Some of the woman's hatred had entered into him, debasing him to her level. He moved to the bureau and grabbed Kate's wrist. When he jerked, she shot forth from the nook, her knees banging against the cot. She fell face down on the hard mattress and lay burrowing her face in the lumpy pillow, trying frantically to cover her body with the bedspread.

"Leroy, scourge her of sin and Satan!"

Crack!

The belt whacked Kate across the buttock. She cried out, a piteous whimper that begged, child-like, for mercy. The belt hit her across the back. "Please, please!" she whimpered for mercy, but there was no mercy here. Twice more, the belt fell. The last time, the end curling around her ribs, biting into one bared breast. The pain was excruciating, but Kate did not cry out. For the first time in her life, she rebelled openly, as wild anger surged through her body.

Like a wildcat, she leaped up. Close to the cot, barring the door, stood her father, the belt upraised. Grinning and drooling, the woman stood behind him, urging him to greater violence.

Outraged, Kate took a single step. She pushed her father and was amazed to find him so weak and powerless that he was shoved out of the tiny pantry. Kate faced the woman. All her stored up resentment propelled the hand that slapped the woman's face.

As her mother retreated, Kate blazed: "You are a sin in the sight of God! The devil has you!"

The woman paused, hatred of Kate naked in her eyes.

"If you touch me again," Kate said bitterly, "I'll scream! I'll fetch the old maids from upstairs! Next door, the Mayberrys will hear, and phone the police!"

Kate pulled the door until it was closed except for an inch of space. "If you come in here again, I'll kill you!" She meant the mother. Kate closed the door, fumbled for a key, but there was no key for this lock.

Panicky, her anger collapsed. She shoved the cot against the door. She braced the cot with the bureau. "To get in," she muttered, "they'll have to break the door down." From the lower shelves, she dragged out a tall canister, wedging it between the bureau and wall.

Gasping for breath, heart thumping, she thought, "They can't get in. Nobody can—get in. If they try to break the door, I'll scream, scream!"

She laughed brokenly.

They can't get in, I can't get out. She said it over and over, then muttered: "Damn them both, damn them in hell's fire, but most of all, damn her!"

Someone knocked on the door.

"Woman," father said.

"Leroy! We'll starve her forth. Then you can scourge sin and Satan from her slut's body, Leroy."

A key turned in the lock. Slow, hateful steps went off. A door closed.

They'll go into the front room, Kate thought. Father will read from the Bible.

Limply, she sat on the edge of the rumpled cot. Damn them for daring to come in here! She became aware of the pain in her bare feet. In moving about, she had walked on broken glass and there were bloody footprints on the floor. Damn her, for daring to snoop in here!

Kate bound a handkerchief around each foot and stopped the trickles of blood.

My blood, she thought viciously. I'll kill her a thousand different ways!

She smiled.

A thousand different ways? That was a line from a poem and that was the way poets wrote.

Chin cupped in hand, Kate sat and thought, and aches stirred in her bruised flesh where the belt had struck.

CHAPTER THREE

OUTSIDE the locked door of the pantry-room, the cuckoo clock in the kitchen began to sound. Kate listened. It was nine o'clock, the cuckoo said.

The window shade had been drawn and the overhead bulb muffled with a towel so that a circle of light shone only on the cot. Making no noise, Kate dressed in the new clothes that Ray Ungas had bought. Underwear, simple dress, and nylon stockings. She hesitated to don the white shoes, decided not to wear them at the moment and pulled the saddle shoes from under the cot. She hid the crisp, new bills inside the top of one stocking.

Mad money, she thought. Plenty of mad money.

Her mind was cold and calm. Time had hardened her to what she must do.

Into the empty handbag, she stowed perfume, lipstick and rouge, handkerchiefs, odds and ends of clothing, toothbrush, and the precious anthology of poems, "Stars To Steer By."

Anything else of value?

Take the dinky maroon hat with the white button, she decided. That will remind you of a high school graduation that you didn't make, *woman!*

Ready?

Nine o'clock, bedtime for the parents. Kate turned off the light. Sound of a footstep? In the kitchen, a loose board creaked.

Knuckles tapped lightly on the door panel.

A whisper filtered through the keyhole and Kate bent down to listen.

"Kate?"

It was her father. Did he have the belt?

"Kate, she's snoring." Pause. "Kate, can you hear me?"

She did not answer, resenting him for the manner in which he had stared at her nudity, hating him for his weakness in not standing up to that woman.

"Kate, I prayed to God alone. Kate, I did wrong. Kate, will you speak to me?"

She did not answer.

Why did he put up with *Leroy* a thousand times each day and countenance the endless nagging, the flood of questions, each one really an order—"Leroy, are you going to scourge her with the strap?" That was monotony. No, hell on earth! All day long, Leroy this, Leroy that.

Did he love that spiteful woman?

No!

Love was giving, not taking. Love was kindness, not nagging. Love was Danny Dorman, not Ray Ungas. Love was tenderness, not a strap.

His slow steps retreated and Kate heard a door close. Later, the soft thud of shoes on the floor, then the creak of bedsprings. Lord, to have to lie beside that woman every night! Kate tiptoed to the window and raised the shade.

The night was dark, but stars were out. Stars to steer by! Somewhere a dog barked. Kate raised the sash. The backyard lay quiet and lonely. On North Street, a horn sounded and a car gunned off.

The window was small. Kate leaned out. It was a long way down to the ground. She let the handbag fall and listened to its thud. Then, one at a time, the white opera pumps.

Kate had no pangs about leaving. Whipping a teenager—no, a grown woman—on the eve of her seventeenth birthday. She sensed not the slightest compassion for the mother who should have befriended her, nor was there in her heart any pity for her father who had proved so weak. Least of all, Kate felt no pity for herself as she faced an unknown future.

If she had done wrong, she was ready to pay fully. You played the game, like sneaking off to Ray Ungas' rooms. If you won, you kept on playing. If you lost, you paid up and no tears at losing. Those were the rules. You thought of number one. Or, you were a sucker. Danny Dorman wasn't a sucker. And Kate Flick wasn't going to remain a sucker all her life.

Leave a note? she wondered.

You have broken my spirit. I go away to die.

Too weepy, like a poor movie.

What about *Goodbye forever?*

Forever sounded corny.

No note, Kate decided. Let them worry about where she had gone. Let them weep for a vanished daughter and fill the space of years with sorrow.

Sorrow and tears?

That woman was beyond tears.

Besides, Kate Flick, you're right. The things you should have had, the things rightfully yours in a rich country, like lipstick and nylons and decent clothes, they denied you. The love they might have given to offset what your eyes craved was completely lacking in a wrecked home. If you needed lovely things to wear, and there was an easy way to those lovely things like loaning your body for a few minutes, then you loaned your body. Don't let Ray Ungas ever get the idea you gave him your heart. Don't let him get the idea that you gave up the right to think, either.

By this devious process of reasoning, Kate convinced herself that what she had done in Ray Ungas' rooms had been a necessary means to a worthwhile end, the gaining of something precious. It had been like loaning an article of wearing apparel to someone in need. Each got what he had wanted and there was pleasure both in giving and receiving.

One point worried Kate. With Ray, there had been instant pleasure in the sex act, like a release of something that had been bottled within her and needed to be let out before she exploded.

She ceased thinking and stared at the ground below the window. Miles down, it seemed, in the shadows. Twisting around, she stuck one foot out the window, and by bracing herself on the bureau, managed to set both knees on the sill. The smallness of the window almost outwitted her since her buttock was still too high to back out.

Well, only one way to do this!

She wriggled and lay flat. A silent fit of laughter shook her. If some neighbor saw a behind emerging from a narrow window! Lord, what a shock! Or view! She began to slide. For a frantic clawing moment, she dangled in space, fingers gripping the sill. Suspended weight overpowered the strength of her arms and she lost a claw-hold on the sill. First the sill, then the weatherboards were brutally raking her breasts, and she landed with a shock that jarred her mind. She lay on the ground, a tumble of arms and legs.

Had *they* heard the crash?

No sound from the silent house. Good!

Kate tested her legs and found them sound. Her back ached, but that was because of the belt. She stood up, took a little leaping step.

Free, free, free! her mind sang. Kate Flick! You're free, of them!

In a spirit of rebellious freedom, she flung the old saddle shoes far into the darkness and rid herself of the last vestige of "kid" clothes. Bag in hand, wearing the white opera pumps, she slipped into the alley next to the Mayberry house.

Lights in their kitchen. Mrs. Mayberry's ample laugh. "Fred, you want another beer maybe?" Good-natured Fred saying: "Yeah, and bring a bottle, Hurry up, wrestling's started." TV and beer and laughter and love next door. For a moment, Kate experienced qualms, remembering the good times she had had next door. If the Mayberrys had only been her parents!

In the front yard, a tomcat slipped along North Street. Kate bent down at the corner formed by porch and wall, and there was the daffodil, catching and reflecting light from the street. *Magnificence,* such a pretty flower.

The name rolled off her tongue with a roller-coaster sound. She picked the flower tenderly, sniffed the trumpet, but found very little aroma. Now, there was absolutely nothing in the house to keep her longer.

At the limit of the Flick backyard, Kate turned for a final glance at the house as it sat in the blackness. She murmured fiercely, "Goodbye," and the word was a brave, tiny sound in the stillness of the night. Like a homeless cat, Kate slipped to the street that paralleled North. When she saw the familiar coupe, she began to run.

Through the lowered window of the coupe, the night breeze siphoned in pleasantly. Outside, the coupe's head-lights bored a tunnel into the darkness and outlined the concrete road. Black trees gushed past, swishing. Then a lonely gas station materialized on the right.

Ray parked on the shoulder beyond the station. "Wait here, kid," he ordered. "I'll only be a sec." He went off and entered a public phone booth.

Kate relaxed in the coupe, twirling the daffodil. She stretched her legs, kicked off the white heels, and sat quietly.

Ray, of course, had been surprised to see her at the coupe with a packed handbag. "You really want to gun off tonight, huh?" he had asked.

"Right now."

"What about—uh, them?"

Kate had explained about the smashed mirror, the awful accusations, and the whipping.

"Kid," he had wondered, "did they learn my name?"

"Of course not. I'm no sap."

"Did they find out about the fifty bucks?"

"It's in the top of my stocking."

"Kid, you never want to see them again?"

"I do not."

"Good." Ray had licked his lips. "Look, I got big things planned for us. Wait an' see just how big, kid."

Ray had driven off, later crossing George Washington Bridge and turning north. A few minutes ago, they had reached open country and Ray had said, "Westchester."

Now steps sounded and Ray slid behind the wheel.

"You phoned?" Kate wondered.

"Yeah, to let 'em know we're on the road." Ray lit a cigarette. "Want a smoke, kid?"

"No." Ray irritated her. "You'd better get one thing straight. Don't call me kid. I grew up in a hurry tonight. At this place in Westchester, you said Danny wanted me to act like a woman. Twenty years old. Remember that."

"Sure." Ray drove off, one hand negligent on the wheel as the coupe gained speed. "So, your old man really busted into your bedroom, huh?"

"He did."

"You naked?"

"Except for panties."

"Jeez! What'd the old goat say?"

"He called me woman."

"I'll bet! You're stacked, kid!"

Kate frowned. "Ray, I asked you not to use that infantile name again."

"Touchy tonight?"

"It's just that I'm no child. And if a man whipped your bare flesh, you'd be touchy, too."

"No man can belt me one," Ray bragged.

From the rear, headlights swarmed up. A car swished past. Twin tailights glittered and hurried ahead.

"A Caddy," Ray grunted. "I'll have one soon."

Traffic was sporadic on the parkway. Kate closed her eyes. She dialed out Ray's conversation.

"Asleep?" he asked, and she did not answer, preferring to keep silence and thus distance between them.

Minutes droned by. Kate's mind idled, content with the present, unconcerned with the future. The air cooled rapidly. Kate yawned, asked: "How much further?"

"Two or three miles to the turnoff."

"The nearest town?"

"Kisco, maybe. Or Brewster."

"How do you know the way?"

Ray laughed. "I got a tip—look, I get around."

Dark, wooded hills loomed on either side. Beyond a railing, a brook tossed up muted music.

"Kate, you happy?"

"Yes, but tired. My back aches and I want to scratch. I hurt myself backing out the window."

"The crazy sonuvabitch." Pause. "But you didn't tell them a thing about me, huh?"

"Stop worrying about yourself."

"Who, me worry?"

"I'm not worried."

Ray hunched over the wheel, patted Kate's thigh. Her legs stiffened.

"Kate. When they find you gone, what will they do?"

"I don't know or care."

"Phone the police?"

Kate countered: "Why phone the police?"

"To notify the Missing Persons Bureau or something. They send out circulars with a description and a pix, kid."

"Don't call me kid again!"

"What's eatin' you?"

"I'm a woman. You said so. Danny Dorman said so. Tonight my father said so. My mother knew it all along. Let them go to the police, they'll never find me and drag be back to that hole! I'm through with them!"

"Good."

Ray flipped a lighted butt out the window.

"I meant to tell you something before. I sold this heap and have to come back to deliver it tomorrow. That's why I can't hang around Westchester. And I'm moving to an apartment in New York any day, now. Uh—I don't want nobody to tie me into you—yet. That might lead to Danny, see?" He grinned sideways, but Kate stared at the concrete up ahead. "I won't be up to see you too often. I got me another job in Manhattan, a damn good job. On weekends, I'll drive up and we'll go to a motel."

"As you say," Kate answered indifferently, but knew she'd rather die than sleep with him again.

The coupe slowed. Ray peered at the shoulder carefully, suddenly braked and the coupe left concrete for a sinuous stretch of black macadam. Thick woods walled them in. Ray kept his eyes on the woods, driving slowly. Then, he cut the wheels sharply and pulled onto a grass-covered lane flanked by bushes and trees. A few feet in, he cut the switch, flicked off the headlights, and night dropped around them like a stone.

"Ray!" Kate leaned forward. "Is this the place?"

"In a way," Ray laughed, a brittle sound. "I been thinkin'. It's been a long time."

"I don't understand."

"Too damn long!" Ray slid across the seat. One thigh rammed Kate hard. "You been puttin' me off lately and me givin' you all the presents. That's not my way. You take from good old Ray, but you don't give much."

Kate waited.

"Look, I ain't a stone!"

"Ray." Kate's voice was a whisper.

"Yeah?"

"Please. Not right now."

"Christ!" His voice was a panted, coarse sound. "Just a little lovin', okay?"

"I—I'm hurt! From the beating and fall!"

A possessive arm gripped her shoulders and pinned her fast Kate shivered. Ray yanked her hard against him. Kate turned to him suddenly, burying her face against his coat. A strong hand pried her chin up. "Don't lie." His voice was a growl. "Jeez, you like it, too." His lips were a wet scorch on her cheeks. The lips then found Kate's and his tongue tried to work into her mouth, but she sat unresponsive.

"What the hell's the matter, huh?"

"Not here!"

His lips shut off her protests and one hand worked under the dress. Kate struggled, pitting her strength against him, but he was the stronger of the two by far. His clammy hand irritated her flesh and she lunged backward. An elbow hit the door latch and pressed it down. The door opened. Kate spilled from the coupe. But Ray was right after her. Again, she tried to wriggle loose, but his hands were steel.

"Ray! For God's sake!"

"Dammit, lie still!"

She would have to wear this dress later. So rather than have him rip it, she suffered him to unloose several buttons and slip it from her body. But once the frock was off, she fought like a wild-cat. This seemed only to excite Ray the more. Sitting on her legs, he tore the bra from her shoulders. Her white, rose-tipped breasts tumbled forth in all their glory, and he bent to fondle them, kiss them. This gave her a chance to kick free, and she leaped to her feet. But he was upon her instantly, flinging himself at her legs like a football tackler, tumbling her to the grassy ground.

In this position he ripped off the scant covering still on the lower half of her body, but did not stop to remove her stockings or shoes. Instead, in a mad slobber of desire, he kissed her thighs, her stomach, her breasts, her lips. Then she became aware of his seeking manhood. She knew she should scream, but she was afraid to. If her screams were heard, it would mean that sooner or later she would come to the attention of the police, and this she could not risk.

No, all she could do was fight her own lone battle here in this isolated darkness. She began to kick again, to wriggle and wrestle and slap. But she was tired, out of breath. And despite herself, the feeling of Ray's hard body was evoking an unbidden response deep inside her.

Not to be denied, Ray was now forcing her to meet the full thrust of his passion. Kate sighed. Hating herself for it, she could not keep from yielding a bit, accommodating him: a moment more, and her body of its own volition moved in full, delicious response. After all, she was being taken, whether she liked it or not. She might as well make the most of it!

With a shuddering sigh, she buried her face in his neck and surrendered to sensation. The bodies, male and female, rocked and writhed. A paroxysm of ecstasy possessed them both—and at last came surcease.

Ray released her.

"Get up," he said curtly. "Dress yourself, kid."

"You stinker," she said. "They don't come worse than you."

"You liked it, didn't you?"

"I couldn't help myself. But that was rape. Just plain rape."

She got into her clothes. Without speaking, they took their places in the car.

Ray drove silently. His face was a white blob of hatefulness to Kate. For the first time, she saw him for what he was, a ratty-faced, avaricious bloodhound who had stalked her. Why, she wondered in despair, had she ever roused the courage to visit his place that first time? He's old. Twenty-eight, Kate Flick. Positively ancient. And a cave-man. If he treated you gently—

Well, it was done.

"Ray." Kate's voice was a small, tight sound inside the coupe. "Were you careful?"

"I lost my head."

"Didn't you—"

"Damn you, there wasn't time! You used to like it, even told me you did!"

Miserably, Kate shrank against the corner cushion. Suppose, she worried, she became pregnant from this brute? Covertly, Kate peeked at him.

She wanted to scratch his eyes out. She thought of grabbing the wheel, twisting, and heading the coupe for the nearest tree.

Quickly, she discarded such a childish idea. This man was a menace, far worse than the brute he had been in the woods.

Kate thought back to that night at Ray's rooms when Danny Dorman had come. Ray had gone out for more liquor. Then, Danny had caressed and kissed her, and it had been so thrilling that she hadn't kept tabs on—well, on things. Only that thin nightgown, then no nightgown, and Danny had been so gentlemanly. Ray had come back too soon, while she was still without the gown.

Ray had made like it was a joke. "So," he had jeered to Danny, "you stole my girl, huh?"

Danny had been drunk. When Ray produced a camera and said, "I'll take a picture for a gag," Danny had blinked.

What had happened next?

Oh, Danny had tried to grab the camera. Danny had sworn at Ray. Or had it been Ray swearing at Danny? No! Both of them swearing and arguing like tomcats on a back fence and she had thought it was over her and—

She had dressed quickly, avoiding both of them. Danny had gone out into the cold night with a hat and overcoat. She had tried to catch up with Danny, but had had no luck.

Danny sending fifty dollars every week?

One night of love. Money. A picture. Ray moving to Manhattan. Talk of a new Caddy and—

"Kid," Ray blurted, "this is it. Stay in the coupe and keep your mouth shut till I come back."

If he calls me a kid again, Kate thought, I'll bash in his ratty face with my heel!

In the reflection of headlights off the macadam, Kate saw a sign: HILL CABINS, ROOMS. Below the main sign was a lighted legend which read: "Sorry, no vacancies."

Ray cut the headlights.

To the left there were signs of habitation—a white picket fence, an open gate and a lane that led to a house well back among several huge elms.

"I'll check," Ray ordered. "She expects you but—"

He let the rest of the sentence hang. He fumbled a roll of bills from a jacket pocket, peeled off three, and thrust them into Kate's hand. They were several twenty-dollar bills. "Now, a Mrs. Wembler runs this—uh, give her that money tomorrow and she can buy you some clothes in the nearest town. And keep your big mouth shut, understand?"

Kate didn't understand. She said coldly: "I'm not to go in town because the police may soon be looking for Kate Flick, North Street, Newark, who disappeared from home—is that it?"

"Yeah."

"Ummm, I'm still not seventeen. You brought me here from Jersey and I'm a minor and—"

Without a word, Ray slapped Kate hard on the mouth.

"Shut up!" he snarled, as she cringed. "You're in this game up to your neck. Up to your bare neck, understand?" He waggled a fist under her nose. "Sit here. Keep quiet. You do what I tell you to do. If you don't, you lose your front teeth."

Ray slid from the coupe.

Kate licked her bruised lips with a dry tongue. Blood salted her tongue and she shivered. If only I were a man for five minutes, she thought bitterly, and clenched her fists. She became aware of the bills. Sixty more dollars? Business-like, she hid the bills with the others in the top of a nylon stocking.

I'm a little fool in a mess, she thought. How do you get out of the mess, little fool?

Her mind began to harden. Why had Ray Ungas been so insistent that she come to this god-forsaken place in the wilderness? "Because of Danny," Ray had said. Why, because of Danny?

Did Danny know the cruel side of Ray Ungas? And who was really doing the running—you or Ray? Ray was worried. Everything he said suggested he was worried. But about what?

Kate peered from the window and saw Ray mount a porch. Pause. A door opened. A woman stood silhouetted against light. The woman greeted Ray, and Kate tensed. Then they went inside and the door closed, shutting off the light.

Why had that woman addressed Ray as "Mr. Adams?"

Everywhere Kate turned there were more puzzles in this game she did not comprehend. Kate slipped from the coupe and kicked off her shoes.

Curiosity drew her to the house, sent her padding across the macadam in stockinged feet. She had to find out, and soon, all she could about this place.

Was it—she searched her mind for a word—a "fancy" house where men found willing women for a price?

Kate shivered. No more men in my life, she decided.

The lush, green lawn muffled her hurried footsteps. She passed under an apple tree covered with blossoms and the air was redolent with their sweetness. At the side of the house, light streamed from an open, rectangular window. Kate crept forward and halted outside the patch of light on the lawn.

"—and I'm the one," Ray was saying, "who tells you how much I pay." His voice had a crisp, dry sound. "I don't give a damn what kind of a place local people think you run, but I know what goes on here. That's my advantage, Mrs. Wembler. Just so you don't get any ideas, remember I know how you work this setup. I'm no sap."

A woman started to protest, but Ray clipped off the argument with: "Don't you try to give me no trouble. More than twenty-five bucks a week is trouble. As for the job, make that a hundred bucks an' be damned glad I shell out. Take it or leave it. No questions asked of the girl. That's it. Leave it and you lose everything. Take it and you still make money."

"You drive a hard bargain, Mr. Adams."

"I hold the high cards. What about it?"

Mrs. Wembler said stiffly: "You give me no choice."

"The hell I don't. You get nothin' but trouble or twenty-five a week an' another hundred."

"That's no choice."

"Stop stalling." Ray laughed nastily. "You're a business woman. You want to keep this business?"

"You're hard on a lonely, defenseless woman!"

Ray sneered: "I'm no soft-bellied sap like the ones you bleed. Do we deal?"

"I'm forced to agree."

"That's smart, Mrs. Wembler. And no questions flung at the girl tonight or anytime. She won't give you trouble. Keep her here, no trips to town. Don't try to welsh, either. You won't get away with it. If you're smart—"

"I wish," Mrs. Wembler interrupted, "that you'd get the hell out of here! Fetch the girl."

Ray laughed.

Kate ran, feather-light, across the lawn. She was out of breath when she reached the coupe and donned her shoes.

Ray Ungas' words had had a terrifying sound. Certainly, he had frightened poor Mrs. Wembler.

In God's name, what was this place?

Why had he brought her here?

Why did he threaten this strange woman?

What was the hundred dollars for? What *job*?

No questions. Don't welsh. Keep her out of town.

It sounded like jail—or worse!

Hurry! Kate thought. You can get away!

She slid into the coupe, closing the door softly. She fumbled for the ignition key, then remembered tardily that Ray had taken the key into the house. She found the handbag on the floor and grabbed it up.

Ray's footsteps crossed the macadam. He opened the door and leaned in.

"Come on," he ordered smoothly. "It's okay to go in."

"Ray! Must I?"

"Yeah."

"I'd rather go with you!" That might be a way to escape from him and this place. "Ray, take me with you?"

Ray reached inside and flicked on a panel light. "Are you scared?" he demanded.

"No," Kate chattered.

"Get out, kid. Shake the lead outa your tail and head for the house. I'll wait till you go in."

She turned away from him, eyes downcast. On the worn rubber floor mat, she spied the daffodil. During the hour with Ray, the flower had slipped from her hand and memory. Now, it lay crushed on the mat. Tears filled her eyes. That beautiful flower, dead, just as she was. She picked up the flower and left the coupe.

Ray grabbed her arm.

"Kid, you listen to me. Don't tell that old bag a thing about us, not even my name. If she questions you, let me know."

Ray gave her a push and Kate stumbled across the macadam.

Her feet were leaden. She breathed shallowly and forced herself to take each step.

To jail, Kate Flick.

Wait—if Ray were moving to Manhattan, how would she be able to let him know about anything that happened here? Suppose Mrs. Wembler were a jailer and—

She walked along the flagstones and reached the porch. From the direction of the coupe, a door slammed. It had a final sound, like a period at the end of a sentence.

When he drives off, Kate thought, I'll run!

She hesitated on the steps, peered at the dim coupe. Drive off, she thought. Hurry, hurry!

The front door opened.

"Don't stand out there all night!" Mrs. Wembler snapped. "Come in, Miss Flick."

Ray told the woman her name, but not his own. Why?

Kate entered a long, lighted, carpeted hallway. The door closed at her back and a lock clicked. Mrs. Wembler touched Kate and Kate turned.

Mrs. Wembler was a large-boned woman, wearing a neat, white dress. Her face had been made up freshly and she wore a string of pearls. Her hair was beautifully curled. She seemed about forty-years old and stood an inch taller than Kate. Her body was heavy-set, but she was not dumpy. She eyed Kate with black, unemotional eyes.

"Good heavens!" Mrs. Wembler exclaimed. "I didn't think that you—why, you're beautiful!"

Kate waited, not knowing what to say.

"How did you get mixed up with—your dress is torn, my dear. And soiled." Mrs. Wembler moved closer, her voice polite and throatily soft. "My dear, how old are you?"

Kate studied the carpet.

"My dear, you've been crying. There is nothing here to hurt you and nothing for you to worry about. Everything will be all right. Your lips are puffed. Did he strike you?"

If she questions you, let me know.

"I'm all right," Kate said miserably.

"Of course you are, my dear. Are you hungry?"

"No."

"Would you like a nice hot bath, eh?"

"Yes."

"My dear, how long have you known you were pregnant?"

The question hit Kate like a blow. A sob escaped from her lips and she swayed.

A strong, friendly arm wrapped around Kate's back. Mrs. Wembler ordered crisply, "This way, my dear," and helped Kate up a curved, carpeted stairway.

CHAPTER FOUR

KATE FLICK stirred restlessly and opened her eyes. Her first confused thoughts were of the pantry on North Street, then her mother and father. It took her a moment to orient herself to the new surroundings, then memories flooded through her mind and she recalled that Ray Ungas had driven off last night and, temporarily at least, she was free from his devilment and threats.

What did Mrs. Wembler's "place" mean?

This was a square, old-fashioned bedroom with a high ceiling, bright with sunlight and wallpaper which had alternate stripes of white and blue. There was a maple bed where she lay, a nearby night table, a bureau and a vanity with amazing triple mirrors. Two wide windows, both open, wore white curtains and blue drapes.

Outside the nearer window, birds argued strenuously, but Kate heard no other sound in the house. A sheet covered her and a blue blanket lay folded across the end of the bed in case the night turned cold. Kate kicked off the sheet and stretched like an aroused kitten.

Last night, Mrs. Wembler had said, "There's nothing here to worry you, my dear," and Kate had been satisfied.

Swinging from the bed, she stood naked on a throw rug. She had slept that way, having brought no nightgown in the handbag. She tripped to a window and peered out. Bees swarmed in a blossoming apple tree whose branches reached the window.

At the edge of a stretch of side lawn was a mass of short-stemmed tulips, solid red with a yellow brim. Beyond a fence of white palings the woods reached off to the lift of several wooded hills. Kate leaned out the window. There seemed to be the corner of a barn out back and beyond that what appeared to be the slanting roof of a cabin, like the ones at motels. Above was the tremendous arch of blue sky, bluer than she had ever dreamed a sky might be, except in a poem.

Gold of the sun. Green of the many trees and fields. Blue of the sky. A glorious gold-blue-green day. Also a red day, for the mass of bright tulips below. Kate drank in the lovely, lonely colors and inhaled languidly. Never had fresh air tasted so sweet.

She faced the triple mirror. The irony of it: driven from home because of a hand-mirror and now all that glass just for her. A mirror was vanity and vanity was sinful in the eyes of the Lord. That was a lot of rot.

Last night, after undressing, she had soaked in a tub of hot water in a bathroom on the upstairs hallway, scrubbing and soaping herself in an unsuccessful attempt to cleanse herself of the hatefulness of Ray Ungas. Now her skin was pink with health, except for a swollen upper lip where Ray had slapped her and several narrow, ugly welts on her back where her father's belt had fallen.

Before Mrs. Wembler had left, Kate had given the woman sixty dollars for clothes and Mrs. Wembler had promised to purchase proper articles of clothing in town but had failed to mention the name of the nearest town.

Does she hate me because I'm here? Kate wondered, remembering Ray's threats. Now, it seemed that Ray had driven a hard bargain last night.

How much did Mrs. Wembler stand to lose each week that she stayed there?

I doubt that Mrs. Wembler hates me, Kate decided, turning away from the mirrors. Last night, the woman had been very kind, had seemed almost sorry for her. In turn, Kate had been so miserable she had almost blurted out, in answer to Mrs. Wembler's question, that she was not pregnant—oh, unless from Ray Ungas last night!

Was this to become a sort of prison? Kate brushed the disturbing question from her mind because Mrs. Wembler did not seem to be a jailer. Hunger prowled around inside her stomach. Kate peeked into the hallway, found it deserted, and made a naked dash into the bathroom.

It was a lovely place with white-tiled walls trimmed in green and the most beautiful fixtures she had ever seen. When she had finished her morning ablutions, Kate dried with the use of a huge soft towel. Again she peeked into the hallway. It still was deserted, but she heard a step on the stairs.

A tall blonde dressed in a loose robe entered the hallway and glimpsed Kate's peering face.

"I heard noise up here," the blonde offered, smiling. "Come on out, I'm Gloria Marden."

The blonde didn't seem like a prisoner. Kate said, "I'm Kate Flick," but she did not leave the bathroom.

"You came last night?"

"Yes. I saw only Mrs. Wembler."

"And that was no treat, I suspect." Gloria walked to the door and her keen eyes examined Kate's figure. "Hmmm, you've got an attractive body, youngster. A bit of surplus weight here and there, but nothing to worry about Yes, not bad at all. Do you model?"

"Oh, no." The casual question puzzled Kate. "Why did you ask that?"

"Because I model. Maybe you should, but it's a rat race, I warn you. Offhand, I'd say you're photogenic, but I'm not a camera." Gloria smiled amiably. "But don't try clothes-horse. You flaunt too much bust and you lack the hungry face. Those bitches in *Vogue* wear falsies because they've less mammary development than an ironing board. Kate, you're the innocent, unspoiled type, so don't try underwear."

"I never thought of modeling!" Kate exclaimed breathlessly. It was so nice to be near a professional model.

Gloria Marden wore blonde hair combed carelessly. She had no makeup on and seemed overweight, but that might be the robe which was very loose. Also, she had seemed short of breath from a trip up the stairs.

"I'm pregnant," Gloria said casually, and shrugged. "Two weeks and I'll be ready to pop, I hope. You?"

Kate flushed furiously.

"Skip it," Gloria added.

"Any men here?" Kate stammered, rather amazed at the blonde's blasé admittances.

"Men?" Gloria's full lips curled. "Thank God, no. It was men who got us here, youngster. Had breakfast?"

"No, and I'm starved."

"In this dump," Gloria explained, "you forage for breakfast. Any kind of juice, bacon and hen fruit, toast, and always plenty of hot coffee. The best thing about the place is the coffee. I suppose you'll eat like a horse in this countrified atmosphere and you'll like it here. I eat like a horse, but I don't like it here." Gloria smiled. "Don't mind the gripes, youngster. I've had two months of ozone and loneliness, and Broadway is a pleasant memory."

"I only brought one dress, which is soiled and—"

"Clothes mean nothing here," Gloria advised. "If you need any things, I've plenty down the hall. I didn't dare leave any of my good stuff in the city apartment. The two hags I room with would have reduced my clothes to rags before I got back from having Junior. Yes, Mrs. Wembler stresses the informal atmosphere and sometimes I feel ready to scream, Kate. Why don't you run downstairs like you are and get something to eat?"

"I'd rather—uh, dress!"

"Suit yourself. The only man here is an old coot named Joe-somebody. He's at least sixty-five and no manhood left, thank God. About all he does is clip the grass and take Mrs. Wembler's orders. What about a robe, darling?"

"I haven't one."

"Follow me to the royal wardrobe. It won't be Sak's, but it's not Gimbel's basement, either."

Kate followed Gloria into a room which was a duplicate of her own, except that the striped wallpaper was white and green.

"Try the closet and take what you need," Gloria advised.

Kate went to the closet.

To be undressed in the presence of another female was rather a novel experience. Although she had been naked with dozens of girls in the shower room at high school, this was different, somehow. Gloria was an older woman. But Gloria was not in the least interested in Kate's nudity.

From many clothes, Kate selected a quilted housecoat in pale green, slipped it on, and knotted the belt. Gloria posed by a vanity cluttered with feminine junk.

"Kate, nobody asks questions in this dump. Except me." Gloria's eyes were guilelessly green. "Sometimes it's better to mind your own business, but it's always choice. Personally, I don't give a damn what people know about me and you can't disguise pregnancy too long. Mind one question?"

"Of course not."

"You have a lovely voice, Kate, and you're rather nice. How old are you?"

Kate liked this strange, amazingly candid woman. "Today," Kate admitted unhesitatingly, "I'm seventeen."

"My God, jail-bait!" Gloria stared. "You and some college kid in this together?"

"I don't understand."

"Don't try. Don't let the fact get around that you're a kid. And forget that I asked. You should pass for twenty. And you can. Oh— if I had nasty welts on my back, I'd ask somebody to paint the welts with iodine. Iodine's antiseptic as hell, but it's smart to be healthy."

"Will you, please?"

"Yes, and pitch that stupid robe. I wear it for confinement, but it fits you like a tent"

Kate took off the robe, still feeling uncomfortable.

"Holler if this hurts," Gloria suggested, unstoppering a dark bottle. "I won't stop painting, but you holler."

In spots, the iodine burned and Kate winced. Afterward, Gloria suggested: "Care for a spot of brandy after the ordeal? It can't hurt and it might help a bit."

"Well—"

"Do you drink, Kate?"

"No, but—" A sudden determination to act more mature overpowered Kate's qualms. "I'll try."

Gloria poured brandy into a tumbler, then half-filled a small shot glass, and handed Kate the latter. Green eyes measured Kate over lifted glasses.

"Did your boy friend slap you last night, Kate?"

"Yes."

"He's a son of a you-know-what," Gloria said cheerfully, and smiled. "Here's to men, youngster. They love you and love loving you, but leave you. We need 'em and we don't need 'em. Whatever we try, we can't win. It's the woman who pays the tab, darling. Here's to manly confusion."

It was hard-boiled talk far beyond young Kate's ken and her limited experience in the field of love, but she accepted what the older woman had said.

Gloria finished the brandy and set the glass carelessly atop the vanity. Kate sipped tentatively. The brandy fired her lips and throat. When it slid into her stomach, she sensed a glow. With a show of bravado, not at all in keeping with her usual conduct, Kate drained the shot glass. Her taste for the brandy had been purely experimental. Gloria seemed preoccupied with her hair as she gazed in the mirror.

I like her, Kate thought warmly. Immediately, she accepted me here and God knows, I needed friendship. She's been around. Every word proves she knows the score. And a man has hurt her very badly, much more than Ray hurt me. Gloria's mature, not rebellious like I am. As I grow older, Kate wondered, will I become less and less rebellious and adapt myself to—well, to the requirements of a more adult life?

"Kate," Gloria suggested, "don't stand there in the nude when the drawers are crammed with stuff to wear."

Kate began rummaging through bureau drawers which were overflowing with lovely things to decorate a woman's body. She chose a white bra, panties and a slip to match.

Gloria walked over and inspected the selections. "Darling, you can learn the tricks at seventeen just as easily as later." Gloria took the slip and bra and returned them to a drawer. "Learn to accentuate the positive, darling. Believe me, you've got it."

Kate slipped into the panties.

Gloria said, "This," and handed Kate a white sweater.

The material was soft to the touch. Kate pulled it over her head and Gloria adjusted it.

Gloria said, "And this," and produced a green skirt. It fitted perfectly.

"Green heels, in the closet," Gloria suggested.

Even the heels fitted.

"Well?" Gloria asked.

Kate stepped to the mirror. The image astounded her. Why—why, already she seemed several years older. The tight sweater gave her a sophisticated allure and the heels added height.

"You're a darling!" Kate cried ecstatically.

"So the man kept telling me," Gloria drawled cryptically. "The hair's all wrong, of course, but we can fix that up later. You've been careless about eating habits, but five or six pounds of surplus weight can be slimmed off. You should exercise properly. If you're interested, I know the routines and—"

A spasm of pain shot through Gloria's body and she shuddered. Her face whitened and she winced.

"Junior's trying to kick his way out!"

Gloria took Kate's hand, opened the robe, and laid Kate's hand on her inflated belly. Something stirred under Kate's palm, then she distinctly felt a slight kick.

"It's alive!" Kate gasped.

"He'd better be, all the trouble he's given me! He must take after his father." Gloria grimaced and Kate withdrew her hand. "They told me the first baby comes any time, but the second one always takes nine months. If I lose my shape because of Junior, I'll murder that man when I get back on Broadway."

"Aren't you married?" Kate blurted out. Instantly, she regretted the thoughtless question that had slipped off her lips. "Gloria! I didn't mean to pry!"

"Who does?" The question had not altered Gloria's poise. "I'm not married, but the father is. And you're not married, either, but don't ask me how I know. In fact, who is married who comes to this place?" Gloria smiled. "And the Wembler woman never was married either, despite the title she sports."

Finally, Kate understood the sort of place to which Ray Ungas had brought her. If unmarried girls in trouble came here, why am I here? Kate wondered. Why did Ray Ungas insist that I come here? What is this game of his?

"Stop feeling sorry for yourself," Gloria advised. "I need more coffee and you need breakfast. Let's go."

Downstairs, the kitchen was immaculate, sunshiny and empty of people. They sat in a cozy breakfast nook by an open window, watching an elderly man who puttered in the vegetable garden.

"Him?" Kate wondered.

"Joe-somebody," Gloria explained. "And a good joe, too. I think he knows where every mouse holes up in this place, but he's intelligent enough to appear to mind his own business. From now on, youngster, I'm going to gad around with octogenarians and eunuchs."

Gloria sipped black coffee, but Kate ate like a starved long-shoreman. Afterward, they wandered outside and sprawled on a blanket in the morning sun near a brook which bordered the Wembler farm.

Gloria had suggested, "Nothing like an all-over tan," and they lay basking in the nude.

It was pleasant on the blanket. The sun was hot and pen-etrating, and Kate could hear the birds chirping in the nearby woods and the steady purling of the brook waters. For the first time since she had arrived at Mrs. Wembler's Kate relaxed, felt completely at ease.

"Youngster," Gloria murmured, "I'm naturally nosy and label it friendship. When did you discover you were in trouble?"

"I think last night."

"The man who brought you here?"

Kate nodded.

"I can understand why he fell for you. Hmmm, I picture him as tall, wide-shouldered, the athletic type. And rather handsome, the type you'd fall for. I like the type, too—if he has any brains in his head. Does your man have plenty of money, Kate?"

Kate hesitated. Ray Ungas? How could she ever bear to tell Gloria about the ratty, insignificant, ancient man who had— *Don't answer questions here!* That had been Ray's admonition. Yet, Kate felt she had known Gloria Marden for weeks, not just a casual hour. Gloria's personality had that sort of impact on a stranger. She must be awfully popular with men, Kate imagined, making them feel at ease with her in an instant. Still, how much should Kate tell Gloria? Not one word of Danny Dorman!

Kate said thoughtfully: "Frankly, I don't know how much money my—uh, man has."

"How can he afford—look, the Wembler woman charges seventy bucks a week just to eat and sleep here, not to mention the extra clips. Finally, there's the doctor who hovers in the background and—are you having the baby or an abortion?"

"Have a baby or an abortion?" Kate said, repeating Gloria's question. "I hadn't thought of that at all. You see, I'm not pregnant."

There was a long pause. Gloria stared at the sky. Then: "Okay, you're a beautiful riddle. Did the man tell you all about your big, beautiful eyes, darling?"

"Yes."

"He wasn't kidding."

With an effort, Gloria sat up, crossing her legs at the ankles. She gestured toward several neat cabins in a row behind a barn that served as a garage.

"Women come and go," Gloria said. "Only two cabins occupied at present and only us chickens in the house. A snooty clothes-horse is here for a check, then an abortion in a day or so.

She'll fade into the night. There's a college girl, also. The cabins suggest they wish to be left alone, so leave them alone."

Gloria chattered steadily, explaining that when a girl learned she was in trouble and consulted a certain Park Avenue doctor, he always asked a simple question: *Do you want the baby or not?* A *no* meant an abortion and a brief sojourn here; a *yes* meant here, too, but a longer sojourn, since this was the doctor's "outlet" and headquarters, as he was careful not to perform an abortion in New York City.

And it was amazing, Gloria continued, how many girls wanted their babies, particularly if the child were the first. The college girl was due in a day or so. Her parents, who lived in Massachusetts, thought she was in Texas for "seminar" study. It seemed the girl had a classmate in Texas and the classmate sent telegrams, never letters, every week to the unsuspecting parents, explaining how much fun she was having in Texas, how awfully busy she was with her work, not to worry about her, and so on.

This was a strange, realistic world into which Kate had been propelled. Pregnant women were commonplace in Newark, the difference being that the women had all been married, as far as Kate had known. It was a shock to learn that a profitable business flourished as the result of girls' unfortunate predicaments.

Kate wondered: "Your first baby, Gloria?"

"And my last." The words had a final sound, like the end of a book. "After the baby is born, they tie something and you've eliminated the risk. I don't want something *tied,* I want it padlocked! Still—" Gloria broke off the thought, lolled on one side. "Dammit, I like babies! If the world weren't such a tough place for a bastard, I'd—never mind!"

Always before to Kate's ears, bastard had been a dirty word, but not as Gloria had used it.

"Youngster," Gloria continued, "I like talking to you. You're a good listener and I like the sound of my own voice. Mrs. Wembler keeps telling me I talk too much, but I explained it was the habit of a lifetime and not easily broken and to mind her own business." Gloria gestured impatiently. "Men are all alike, taking only what they need from you. You're lucky, I suppose, if they have the money to pay the piper. I was lucky and unlucky."

Kate sensed a story in the offing and listened attentively. Gloria did not disappoint her.

"Take that man who fooled me, Kate. He was rich and handsome, on the make, but did I know at first that the no-good was already married?" Gloria's stomach jumped and she breathed hard. "Quiet, Junior. You're more fuss than your old man. So, there I was in the big city, a girl from a quiet Ohio farm where the birds and bees are active. But the farm animals condition you to the facts of procreation. I knew the score, and so on. I'd been traveling around for three years. I'd had plenty of dates and knew all about men, I thought. I necked and drank plenty, but I knew how to neck and drink safely. I knew how to take care of myself, what the limits were, and all the precautions and devices to offer a man plenty, but never quite let him get plenty."

Gloria lit a cigarette, inhaled deeply.

"The camera told me I could model and I did staid stuff mostly, but enough of the flimsies to know what it's like. So, I met this no-good on a job, learned later his father owned a big department store over in Jersey. I lived well, I suppose, but I wanted out from the two hags with whom I roomed. At twenty-three, I felt like a homeless cat. I'd had almost everything that a girl could want—good clothes, good times, loving, but I was ready for a husband with money and love tossed in to make it a dream come true."

Without missing a cadence, Gloria continued: "Another fisherman's coming up the brook, either for trout or staring. Old Joe says a good angler can land a mess of rainbow from that rill, but sometimes all they're after is a view of one of us." Gloria playfully patted Kate's bare behind. "Don't panic, youngster. Your essential parts are covered and I don't care one damn. The brook's a barrier, so relax."

Kate, however, squirmed on the blanket. If a strange man's eyes were on her, she thought, it was not right.

"Gloria, if he stares, why aren't you bothered?"

"Because nudists have the right approach to the body. Nakedness is nasty only if you think it so and I don't. Besides, I've been photographed in practically nothing so often, I'm callous. Most top photographers are men who've seen so much flesh they have an objective attitude. They teach you to become objective. And that fisherman can stare at my bare skin all he wishes because some guy staring never made a gal pregnant. Let's see—I answered a call to model girdles, sort of a private deal, only three of us. Me in the girdles, a woman salesman, and this big, handsome no-good with polished manners and eyes. I didn't mind the exposure. It was business and I always tried to earn my money. You learn that the figure inside the garment usually sells the garment. That's good for the client, the agency and the model. About a week later, this no-good began to send flowers and candy, then expensive gifts. To make a stupid story understandable, I liked the guy when he came around everyday—and every night. We fell in love. We were going to marry and we couldn't wait. We were very good together and I'd be a liar if I said I didn't enjoy him. We were happy, full of plans. I missed a couple of periods, but I wasn't worried because he wasn't worried, then he didn't come around for a week and I was worried as all hell. So, I learned he had a wife who'd run off to Reno for a quicky-divorce, changed her mind because she learned about me and—"

Gloria called out: "Hey, mister! Somebody cleaned out all the trout yesterday! Or don't you mind?"

Timidly, Kate peered over a bare shoulder. She glimpsed a face shaded by an old felt hat and wide shoulders above bushes on the opposite side of the brook. Kate reached for the nearby green skirt and pulled it across her buttock.

"Why didn't you tell me sooner?" the fisherman asked.

"I didn't know why you were hanging around!"

"Wasting my time like this," the fisherman grumbled.

"You didn't waste all your time, mister! See you tomorrow!"

The man grumbled unintelligibly and disappeared.

"He'll go home, give his wife a hard time tonight, and she won't know we're the reason." Gloria laughed. "So no-good's addled wife changed her mind about divorce and returned home to stay. I think no-good lacks guts, but there I was way overdue and sick with worry and disappointment. Anyway, Hector did the right thing and steered me to this Park Avenue doctor." Gloria's smooth brow wrinkled in puzzlement. "Dammit, how could a guy named Hector fool me?" Gloria lit another cigarette. "Hector gave me more than an adequate sum of cash, folded his tent, and vanished into the department store business. Kate, don't weep for me. I played and I liked the playing. I lost and I have to pay up, exclamation point. Anything on your mind, youngster, or shall we get dressed?"

"My skin seems scorched."

"Okay." Gloria's smile was brief and detached. "Let's take Junior for a walk."

Junior?

Kate asked curiously: "You're sure it's a boy?"

"Yes, the way he kicks. You see, his old man was a football player. I think it was for Yale."

They dressed and wandered toward the cabins. A girl on the porch of a cabin glanced up, looked away without recognition, and reached for a cocktail shaker.

"Snooty clothes-horse," Gloria hissed. "So damn flat-chested she can't tell in which direction she's headed without consulting a mirror."

A brunette in the opposite cabin sat by an open window and she smiled. Gloria offered: "When's the big moment?"

"Tonight, I understand. I'm built wrong, so it's Caesarean." The brunette's face clouded. "Besides, the parents plan to visit Texas next week and—" The brunette turned away.

"Keep a stiff upper lip, darling," Gloria advised. "You can't take it with you—good luck."

They passed on and Gloria murmured: "She's scared, but the doctor's top-notch, and she'll be all right."

Something that Gloria had said began to bother Kate. "What did you mean, can't-take-it-with-you?"

"Figure of speech. Uh—euphemism, I suppose."

In retrospection, it seemed to Kate that weeks had elapsed since she had fled from North Street, yet it had been a matter of only a few hours. More and more, she liked Gloria Marden. The woman was a window opening on an unsuspected world. Yet Kate was not ready to speak frankly to Gloria.

Reticence? she wondered. Timidity?

Neither, Kate decided. You're ashamed of Ray Ungas.

She had been stupid ever to associate with such a crumb and could not confess the details. But to relate that one precious moment with Danny Dorman—but Danny's name must never be mentioned to Gloria Marden or to anyone!

Near the barn, an expensive new ranchwagon stood parked on the graveled driveway.

"Wembler's back from Kisco," Gloria sneered. "Probably in one hell of a temper, too. It's the cook's day off and Mrs. Wembler hates to cook and serve paying guests."

Mrs. Wembler, as if on cue, appeared at the rear door of the house. She seemed remote in a modish blue dress and blue heels. "Miss Marden," she called out, "may I speak to you a moment?"

"For a moment," Gloria agreed. "See you at lunch, Kate."

Gloria walked on, but Kate turned to the left to inspect a bed of tulips.

Although Kate did not count them, there must have been over two hundred blooms in the bed. There were five separate splotches of color, blending beautifully. Glowing red tulips at the far end of the bed, deep yellow next to the red, then white in the middle, something verging on blue next, and the nearest type red flamed with glowing yellow or maybe it was yellow flamed red.

Steps crunched across the gravel, and Kate turned.

It was Joe-somebody, wearing glasses and work clothes. Gray hair peeped from under an old hat and his blue eyes were keen and alert, although his step was slow.

Joe said politely: "You like flowers, miss?"

Miss. Joe-somebody knew his way around.

"They're so lovely," Kate said. "Those yellow darlings at the end, flamed red. Do they have a name?"

"All tulips have a name, miss. Usually, a proud name, but sometimes an appropriate name. Those are *Prince Carnival*. In olden days, a carnival was a season of merry-making before Lent, a last fling for the fasting period that preceded Easter. Yellow and red—bright, happy colors, miss." Joe's eyes were polite, yet Kate seemed to sense a keen mind at work behind the eyes, a mind brimful of knowledge. "You come talk to me, miss, and I'll tell you all about spring flowers." Old Joe lowered his voice, indicated the house with a head nod. "*She* doesn't know a tulip from a daffodil, but I don't care what she likes. Those tulips are mine, bought and paid for with wages I more than earned, but that's another story."

"Daffodils," Kate mused, remembering the bloom she had picked on North Street and where it was now, crushed and fading, inside the book of poems, "Stars To Steer By," "Joe, at home I had a lovely daffodil, *Magnificence.* Do you have any here?"

"No, but I grew them once." Joe's blue eyes seemed to come alive with the memory. "There's a better sort, miss. *Unsurpassable,* the finest daff ever developed in Holland. Huge blooms with a long, flared trumpet. You have a minute to spare?"

"I have weeks!"

"Sure, you all do, 'cept those in a hurry." Joe grinned. "No offense, miss. I like anything that grows—tulips, vegetables, trees, people, fruits, and babies." His face was kindly, not one bit cold, but Kate noticed that the blue eyes seemed clouded. "Anytime you want to see my Unsurpassables, I'll show them to you. If you'd like flowers for your bedroom, you pick out the ones you want and I'll—"

Mrs. Wembler called from the back door: "Joe, you didn't bury yesterday's garbage yet."

"I didn't?" He seemed amused. "And I didn't bury day-before-yesterday's garbage, either. In fact, I never bury the garbage every day."

"Bury it now!"

"Yes, ma'am. Oh—you mind if I take time off from work to eat my lunch?"

Mrs. Wembler ignored the question. "Miss Flick, may I speak to you a moment?"

At the door, Mrs. Wembler smiled warmly and offered: "Only a minute, my dear."

Kate stepped inside.

CHAPTER FIVE

THE room seemed to be Mrs. Wembler's headquarters. The walls were painted light blue and the woodwork white. Venetian blinds shut out the sun and dark blue drapes, thick and heavy, were in place if anyone decided to cover the blinds. There was wall-to-wall carpeting, a desk, several chairs, a small filing cabinet in one corner, and a portable typewriter on a side table. Only one lamp was on and this cast a cone of light on the desk covered with a spotless blue blotter. The desk lay bare except for Mrs. Wembler's military handbag which she had dropped carelessly before sitting down on a chair equipped with rollers.

What had interested Kate Flick most about this room had been the open door into a dark room off the office. In fact, there were two doors into that room; one which opened into the office and whose edges were bound with felt strips, the other on the opposite side of the jamb, which led into the darkened room. Before Mrs. Wembler had closed one door, Kate had glimpsed a white enamel cabinet and had noticed a faint, antiseptic smell, which she fancied might be from lysol. If there were "operations" performed in this house, were they accomplished in this other room?

Kate sat quietly across from Mrs. Wembler and just outside the cone of light.

"How do you like my place," Mrs. Wembler asked politely, "now that you see it in daylight?"

"It's rather nice," Kate said honestly. "I like the country and the flowers are beautiful."

"You need not be worried or concerned here, my dear. Did you eat breakfast?"

"Yes."

"With Miss Marden?"

Kate nodded happily. "She's been very kind. I ate very well and Gloria had coffee."

"*Gloria* so soon, my dear?"

"She doesn't mind."

"And she was talkative, of course?"

"Yes."

Mrs. Wembler folded her hands atop the desk. Kate noticed two rings on the correct finger, a platinum wedding ring and a sparkling diamond, and wondered curiously why Gloria Marden had been so certain that Mrs. Wembler had never been married.

"My dear," Mrs. Wembler offered politely, "I purchased a few things for you to wear and left them in your bedroom. You will find receipts for each article and the change, two dollars and seventy cents on the vanity. Really, it's quite an accomplishment for a woman to return from a shopping tour with some money unspent! I hope you'll like the clothes, but you must understand that your position here is somewhat unusual, not quite comparable to that of the other guests. However, you seem intelligent and should be able to adapt yourself to the situation. I notice that the clothes you are wearing were not in your handbag last night and presume that Miss Marden has been generous with some of her things?"

"Yes."

"Really, she's quite a dear, not the slightest trouble. You'll not need to borrow from her again, of course." As if in afterthought, Mrs. Wembler added politely: "If your Mr. Adams should telephone, and I'm not here, please tell him that he may phone, but not visit. I forbid the presence of men on my property at all times, except as I have need for a plumber or someone like that. Your Mr. Adams must be no exception to my rules. Is that understood, my dear?"

Kate nodded. This was more than she had expected—Ray Ungas or *Mr. Adams* not able to come here as he wished. That was one way to keep him at arm's length.

"My dear, do you care for a cigarette?"

"No thanks."

"You smoke?"

"A little, but not a habit."

"Everyone has some habits," Mrs. Wembler purred. "Will you pardon my one minor vice?"

"Of course."

There might have been a double meaning in Mrs. Wembler's words, but Kate had detected no sarcasm.

Mrs. Wembler made a little ceremony of extracting a gold case from the handbag, tapping a cigarette on the blotter, lighting up from a gold lighter, inhaling and blowing smoke expertly in twin streams through her nose, before setting the cigarette carefully on a copper ashtray.

"Miss Flick, are you acquainted with the arrangements that your Mr. Adams made for you?"

Kate answered promptly, "No," not wishing to reveal that she had overheard the argument last night.

"Did your Mr. Adams—ah, mention how he happened to know about my place?"

"No."

"Are you or he familiar with this area?"

"I'm not, but I don't know about Mr. Adams. Ummm," Kate remembered, "he had no difficulty in finding your place and drove directly here."

"My dear, before last night, had you the slightest idea that I existed?"

"No."

"Please don't mind my questions! To you, then, I was just a name?"

"Not even a name until last night." Kate leaned forward and smiled. "You've been awfully kind to me, Mrs. Wembler. I want to thank you for doing my shopping."

"Thank you, my dear. Ummm, suppose we come to the point. How freely did you talk to Miss Marden?"

"It was the other way around."

"Yes, I suppose it was. Miss Marden likes to chatter and sooner or later—never mind that!" Mrs. Wembler seemed to undergo some important, inward change, but Kate could not make out what the change was, and forgot about it as Mrs. Wembler continued to talk politely. "I stress the informal atmosphere here, but there are some rules. I must suggest that you not mingle freely with the other guests. Until you become more acclimated to our mode of living and the strict absence of men, why not stay in your room for a day or so—umm, until your Mr. Adams has telephoned. Your meals will be served upstairs and you will have adequate time to consider your—ah, particular problem and make some intelligent decision regarding that problem. How old are you?"

The casual question had been skillfully inserted. Had it not been for Gloria Marden's warning not to mention her age under any circumstances, Kate might have been caught off-guard.

"I'm twenty," Kate said.

"And your home address, my dear?"

Wanting absolutely no link with her past on North Street, Kate countered quietly: "When Mr. Adams made the arrangements, didn't he leave an address?"

"He mentioned New Jersey."

"I live in New Jersey, Mrs. Wembler."

"With millions of other residents, eh?"

"Yes."

"Which is your privilege, of course. Now, I must speak more frankly with you." Mrs. Wembler's hands lay calmly on the blue blotter, the smoking cigarette ignored on the tray. "Your Mr. Adams, whoever he proves to be, is responsible for the situation in which I cannot regard you as a normal guest in this house. Whether or not you understand the arrangements, I have no sure way of ascertaining, but you did not know my name nor know of my place until you came here last night?"

"That's correct."

Mrs. Wembler shrugged. "Please stay in your room, my dear, until your Mr. Adams phones. You may go."

Stay in your room sounded like a jail sentence. Had Ray Ungas suggested that?

Kate hesitated. She knew that Ray Ungas had driven a hard bargain with Mrs. Wembler last night. Already, Gloria Marden had confirmed that knowledge by remarking casually that the weekly rate was seventy dollars, not twenty-five. Kate wanted to blurt out that she hated Ray Ungas or Mr. Adams, never wanted to see him again, and would be pleased if he would drop dead or at least fade from sight. Also, Kate wanted to assure Mrs. Wembler that she would be no problem here, particularly with Gloria Marden, but how could she make such explanations now without Mrs. Wembler asking further questions which must remain unanswered until Kate was thoroughly familiar with what Ray Ungas was up to?

Where, exactly, did Danny Dorman fit into the picture? Why would Ray Ungas phone soon? Would Danny phone? Did Mrs. Wembler know of Danny Dorman?

Perhaps, under the circumstances, it would be smart to stay in the bedroom as Mrs. Wembler had suggested. Then, after several days of thought, it might be possible to slip from this house, run off, and escape from Ray Ungas, also.

Mrs. Wembler picked up the cigarette, inhaled deeply, then viciously snubbed out the cigarette. "My dear," she said softly, "why don't you take your troubled thoughts up to the bedroom?"

Kate rose and turned to the door.

Mrs. Wembler said: "Turn around, you bitch!"

It was a bitter denunciation and an angry order. In amazement, Kate wheeled to face the desk, eyes blazing. At sight of the change in Mrs. Wembler, Kate instantly forgot the hot retort that was ready on her lips.

The polite mask which had covered the woman's strained face had disappeared. There was no possibility of misunderstanding her emotion. Sparks of hate flew from the woman's eyes, a vicious hate such as Kate had seen in her mother's face only last night. Mrs. Wembler's lips were pursed in a single rigid line. A vein pulsed on the left side of a suddenly reddened neck. Her body seemed charged with insidious electricity.

"You bitch!" Mrs. Wembler repeated between her teeth. "This room is sound-proofed!"

Kate stared. Sound-proofed?

Sweat from the woman's working hands had leaked on the blue blotter. She jerked the desk drawer open, pawed inside. When her hands emerged, the left held a tiny nickel-plated revolver which she laid on the blotter.

"Your Mr. Adams," she snapped, "will phone soon or so he intimated last night. When he phones, I will make a date with him for you away from my house. If he dares come here again, I am prepared to shoot him. I will shoot him like the rat he is and feel no compunction. Tell him exactly what I am telling you. Tell him about this gun which I will carry at all times and tell him—"

The angry woman had machine-gunned the words. Running out of breath, she trembled to a stop.

"Damn him!"

From the open drawer, she withdrew an oblong cardboard box which she dropped with a hollow thud on the desk and Kate watched in frantic apprehension.

Was this woman insane? Kate wondered.

"Tell him I don't bluff!"

Mrs. Wembler finally opened the box, which contained cartridges. She broke the revolver and slid a live cartridge into the empty, exposed cylinder.

"I've handled guns since I was ten years old!"

One by one, Mrs. Wembler inserted cartridges until the revolver contained six.

"I can hit a bull's-eye at thirty yards! With this tiny gun, tell him!"

She fumbled the cylinder back into place and laid the loaded revolver on the blotter, then dropped the box of cartridges into the desk drawer, not bothering to close the lid. She slammed the drawer violently, but only a soft, explosive sound, more muffled than clear, was heard in the room.

"The dirty sonuvabitch!" she hissed. "The dirty, blackmailing sonuvabitch! Threatening an honest business woman! The— the dirty *man!*"

Man sounded like a curse word.

When Mrs. Wembler stood erect, she slammed the chair backward and it crashed against the wall.

"Get out, you bitch!"

Terror such as she had never known before gripped Kate and rooted her to the rug. Her eyes clung in fascination to the silver-plated revolver which lay like a deadly menace on the sweated-stained blotter.

A gun, a gun! In God's name, why a gun?

Her mind refused to function.

Mrs. Wembler opened the military handbag, dropped the gun inside, and closed the bag with a click. She set the strap over one shoulder and the bag dangled against one hip, the gun within easy reach.

Mrs. Wembler smiled. Instantly, anger was gone. Again, she was the poised, polite woman whom Kate had first encountered in this house.

"Please go to your room, my dear," Mrs. Wembler whispered. "Stay there—until he phones."

She had spaced the final words, but there was no mistaking the threat if Kate dared disobey. Mrs. Wembler rounded the desk, touched Kate's elbow. Kate shrank back, but Mrs. Wembler's touch had been soft, reassuring.

Mrs. Wembler urged Kate to the door, opened it. She murmured, "So nice to chat with you, my dear," and gave Kate a slight nudge on the back.

Terrified, Kate Flick fled blindly upstairs.

CHAPTER SIX

I N THE SAFETY of her bedroom, Kate breathed hard, more from the continuing terror of the revolver than from the frantic scampering up the stairs.

As she mulled over the scene, gradually gaining control of her emotions, Kate realized that something in Mrs. Wembler's office had not rung true. What had been off-key? More carefully, Kate relived the scene.

The gun had been real enough. So had the cartridges. Kate knew they were "live" cartridges capable of killing because she had seen guns and cartridges next door at the Mayberrys. The gun in the military handbag. Why, this was melodrama! In truth, Mrs. Wembler had played the scene poorly, overdoing the threatening, as if Ray Ungas might be scared through an intermediary.

And it was Mrs. Wembler who had been most scared. Remember how her fingers trembled so that she had had difficulty inserting the cartridges into the cylinder of the revolver? Her fingers had been thumbs! Her fingers had perspired so freely that the revolver had been moistened and more perspiration had dripped from her hands to stain the once immaculate blue blotter.

Two people scared in that office!

Last night with Ray Ungas, Kate remembered further, Mrs. Wembler had been scared rather easily. How quickly she had agreed to Ray's unreasonable terms, saying she had no choice but to accept a stranger's proposition.

Blackmailer, Mrs. Wembler had labeled Ray, a blackmailer threatening an honest business woman. But how "honest" was this vengeful woman?

The fact that Mrs. Wembler was terrified of Ray Ungas did not disturb Kate half so much as the thought that if Ray had blackmailed here so casually he might be pursuing blackmail elsewhere. In the coupe last night, Ray had carried a roll of bills. Was the source of his sudden wealth the result of some scheme against Danny Dorman?

Kate did not know, but she knew what blackmail was, having read about it in the papers. A person threatened someone with public exposure for some wrong and called off the threat only if he were paid tribute in return for silence. Deeply disturbed, Kate mulled the puzzle.

What about the picture Ray had snapped?

At the time, the picture had seemed some kind of joke. Now, she wondered if the picture were the basis for a threat. If it were, then she was—well, like a pawn in this dangerous game. Ray had said simply, evading further questioning: "This is a game and Danny Dorman lost. Like in craps, the loser has to pay up and that's it."

If Ray were a threat to Danny's security, how could Danny be saved? And Danny must be saved at all costs! If the picture were the cause of this entire game, how could Kate retrieve the picture without hurting Danny further?

I can't run from Ray, Kate decided. He's the key to the puzzle.

Hopelessly bewildered, she flung herself prostrate on the bed, careless of the borrowed clothes and unaware that her body mashed several boxes of clothes which Mrs. Wembler had purchased in Mt. Kisco.

"Fool," she sobbed. "You utter fool!"

Time passed, then someone knocked on the door. Kate arose and opened the door. A tray sat on the hallway floor, filled with silver, food on exquisite chinaware, a linen napkin, pack of cigarettes and matches—and a note. Hurriedly, Kate carried the tray to the vanity. A click sounded.

Click?

Barefooted, Kate sped to the door and tried the knob. The knob turned, but the door did not open. Click of key locking the door; that's what she had heard. Yes, she was a prisoner! But what could she do about it?

Kate read the note. The message said, "Stay in your room until he phones. I will talk with him. Oh—I left a sleeping pill for you. Do not take it now, but reserve it for tonight." Kate shredded the note, dropped the pieces in a waste basket. She found the sleeping pill, studied it a moment, then hurled it out the window.

I'm not a prisoner here, she decided. All I have to do to escape is rip up a sheet, knot the lengths together, and slide out the window. I might even jump and grab hold of the tree. If I wish, I may leave any time.

Yet, she knew that she would stay. Ray had moved to Manhattan and she had no way of finding him again until he phoned and she talked to him. And she must keep contact with him if she were ever to see Danny again.

A pleasant fragrance tickled her nostrils and she turned to the loaded tray. Mrs. Wembler had prepared a steaming bowl of thick soup, a charred chunk of steak that exuded rich juices, a green salad, pot of tea, and a dish of lime gelatin topped by a full inch of whipped cream. Kate wasn't the least bit hungry, but she began to eat anyway and soon discovered that her appetite had returned.

The soup was delicious. The steak melted in her mouth. The salad made her long for a second helping, if one had been available. When she had finished the delicious meal, Kate decided to have her first cigarette. She opened the pack and lit one. Imitating Gloria Marden, she inhaled deeply. The smoke filled her lungs, almost gagging her. Disillusioned by the brief experience, she snubbed out the cigarette.

Mrs. Wembler called smoking her minor vice?

Well, there were major vices, too. Like blackmailing. Or threatening somebody with a loaded gun. Or sneaking into a man's room and exchanging one's body—no, lending one's body in return for some clothes.

What about the tray?

When Mrs. Wembler unlocks the door to recover the tray, why don't I attack her? Kate thought.

She was stronger than her father, she knew, but not so strong as Ray Ungas who had—why, he had raped her last night in the woods! Raped a teenager. Raped "jailbait." No wonder he was keeping her here.

Am I stronger than Mrs. Wembler? Kate wondered. Not if she whips out a gun.

Kate shrugged and sat by the window, chin cupped in hand, and listened to the incessant droning of the busy bees in the flowering tree. The bees played a game, too. They gathered the ingredients to make honey in the hive. They served a queen—for free. Stupid bees!

Tired of listening to the bees, Kate found her book of poems and began to read aloud. After a few minutes, even the poetry sounded dull. She leaned back in the chair, closed her eyes …

She awakened with a start. The sun was much lower in the west, she noted. Then someone said: "My dear."

Startled, Kate half-rose from the depths of the chair.

Mrs. Wembler stood in the middle of the room, the military handbag draped over one shoulder and a forefinger to her lips. "I'm sorry that I made such a silly scene downstairs," Mrs. Wembler began humbly. "In truth, I was—ah, upset by the circumstance of your Mr. Adams. Will you forgive me, please?"

Kate shrugged. "Okay."

"Thank you, my dear." Mrs. Wembler smiled. "Oh, Mr. Adams just phoned. At six o'clock, you are to walk west along the road and meet him, as he is anxious to see you. And please relay my message to Mr. Adams."

Mrs. Wembler picked up the tray.

"Miss Flick, of your own free will, you need not stay in this house one moment longer than you wish. I shall not lock the door again. You are free to leave—with your Mr. Adams if you think that best."

Mrs. Wembler left.

One moment, Kate thought, I'm virtually a prisoner in this room. The next minute, I'm free to leave, to do just as I wish. Sure, free to fall back into Ray's grubby arms.

Why, as soon as Ray had phoned, had her status here undergone such an abrupt change?

The question only deepened the mystery.

Suppose, Kate mused, she decided to leave with Ray Ungas. She would be close to him, close enough perhaps to wangle some information, find out if he had some sort of hold on Danny Dorman. What else? Be temporarily sentenced to bed with a man she detested.

If she delivered Mrs. Wembler's threat, how would Ray react?

No, she wouldn't tell Ray about that revolver. Instead she would suggest a rendezvous with Ray in the house. And Kate would be sure to inform Mrs. Wembler of his coming. If the woman is as frightened as she appears to be, Kate thought, she may even kill him. And if she does, Kate Flick will be only too happy to help her dig a lonely grave for him!

It was an utterly ridiculous idea, but Kate liked it and smiled.

Then her face sobered as she realized that soon she must go west along the road to meet Ray. They would be all alone and—Kate shivered. No! Never that again with Ray Ungas.

The more she thought of this inexplicable situation, the more one item puzzled her. Why had Ray felt it was so necessary for her to leave home on North Street and flee to this lonely place in the Westchester hills? The facts were that Mrs. Wembler operated a place for pregnant, unmarried women and Kate was not yet pregnant—she hoped!

Why had Ray brought her here in the first place? Was this his means of hiding her until he found out if she were pregnant? If she were, what would he do about it?

Would her father report her disappearance to the Newark police; and would they attempt to find her?

Suppose the police were to trace her to Mrs. Wembler's establishment, and were then able to connect her to Ray, would Ray be in trouble? After all, she was jail-bait.

The more that Kate viewed the problem, the more she became confused by the endless string of unanswered questions. She simply did not have enough information to solve one question, let alone the entire riddle. But, she wasn't pregnant. And she wouldn't become pregnant from Ray if hoping and praying could avert pregnancy. If she were pregnant, Kate decided, she would have the baby, not submit to an abortion.

Ray Ungas, the threat.

Suppose he did go to the local police with the information that Mrs. Wembler harbored pregnant, unmarried girls who had their choice of babies or abortions? What would the police do to these poor girls?

And what did a girl in trouble do? Go to the Mrs. Wemblers.

Gradually, one idea began to dominate Kate's conscious thoughts. Meeting Ray Ungas at six o'clock, a necessity if she were to help Danny Dorman, presented a problem.

Gloria Marden?

That was a hope!

Kate opened the door and listened. Downstairs a snatch of muted music over a radio and the rattle of dishes suggested that Mrs. Wembler was busy in the kitchen. The sound of a whirring lawn mower meant Joe-somebody was doing a chore.

Kate tiptoed along the hallway and reached Gloria's door. Should she knock? No, because noise might alert Mrs. Wembler. Go right in, she decided.

Quietly, Kate turned the knob, cracked the door open, and stepped inside. The room seemed deserted, then a muffled sob sounded. Kate peered around the door and saw the bed where Gloria lay, feet toward the door, her face buried in a pillow. Some strong emotion shivered Gloria's shoulders and sobs escaped from the pillow.

The sobs reached right to Kate's heart, but she knew better than to attempt to comfort a woman who cried alone.

Glad of her silent entrance, Kate backed from the room and eased the door shut.

Poor Gloria!

Kate stole back to her room and the minutes passed. Finally, shortly after five o'clock, Kate returned to Gloria's door and tapped lightly.

Gloria said, "Come on in."

The rumpled bed had been straightened and a bedspread covered the pillow. Gloria sat relaxed in a deep chair by the open window, smoking a cigarette. A book lay unopened on her lap. Her hair had been freshly combed and makeup brightened her face.

"Yes?" Gloria asked, and her voice sounded distant.

"I have to talk to you."

"And?"

"It's very urgent."

"Well?"

"Gloria, I'm in trouble! I—I don't know where to turn!"

"Why come in here?"

"You're the only friend I have!"

"And what makes you think I'm friendly?"

"You loaned me clothes. You—"

Gloria said quietly: "And you're not pregnant?"

"No."

"Then why come here?"

"I—I don't know, really I don't!" The sudden reversal in Gloria's attitude troubled Kate no end. "Gloria, you've changed! What happened? Is there something wrong?"

"Frankly, there is." Gloria's eyes hardened. "If there's one kind of person I hate, it's a snoop."

She knew I came in without knocking, Kate thought.

"God, to think how I unloaded my brains to you, spilled the whole setup, even told you about the others! You drank in every word and played so innocent!" Gloria leaned forward. "What do you and your man want from us—money? I for one won't give you a dime. You can shout your loudest to the police, or to anybody, but you get nothing from me. Get out before I lose my temper."

Gloria stirred in the deep chair. She brought out a white slipper, holding it firmly.

"Snoop, get out of here before I bash your brains out and let 'em trickle on the rug! That is, if you've got any brains in your empty head!"

"Who told you I was a snoop?"

"Mrs. Wembler." Gloria brandished the shoe. "If I scream, Mrs. Wembler will come on the run. Get out, snoop."

"Gloria! You've got to help me!"

"Ha, that's a laugh."

"Please!" Kate was on the verge of tears at the unexpected treatment. "She threatened me with a gun!"

"Who did?"

"Mrs. Wembler!"

"Say that again—more slowly."

"Mrs. Wembler spoke to you, then she called me into her office. She brought out a gun and loaded it. Gloria, I was scared stiff! A loaded gun!"

"Kid," Gloria suggested, "come here."

Kate stepped closer.

"Sit down."

Kate sat on the floor.

For a moment, Gloria studied Kate's face and the tears in her eyes. "Dammit, I was always taking care of stray cats and dogs on that Ohio farm!" Gloria shrugged. "You're only seventeen?"

"Today."

"Does Mrs. Wembler know that?"

"I told her I was twenty."

"And you're jail-bait, I told you before. Anybody, man or woman, who fools around with you can land in jail. Do you understand that, kid?"

"So that's what's behind this!"

"Behind what?"

"Why Ray—I mean Mr. Adams, brought me here!"

"This Adams—he didn't bring you here to snoop on me and the other girls?"

"I swear to God I'm no snoop!"

"Someone slapped your face last night before you came here and welted your back with a strap. Adams?"

"Yes."

"Why?"

"He didn't whip me, only the slap."

"I'm no mind reader, youngster. If you're in trouble, and not from pregnancy, you'll have to speak out."

At first, Kate went over it hesitantly, starting from the moment that she had met Ray Ungas by the corner candy store on North Street. In telling the story, Kate felt better and hurried on with it, reaching the point of her first visit to Ray Ungas' rooms in the late winter.

"I didn't realize," Kate said earnestly, "why he wanted me there and what he—"

"Skip it. The laws are written to protect kids like you. Ray Ungas knows that. Get on with the story."

Kate told about the acquisition of new clothes, how Ray had broken his promise not to enter the bedroom, that she had never been kissed by a man before, that she was starved dry for love—and nice clothes. Kate told about home, father and mother, and the eternal reading of the Bible, but no application of the Bible's principles in the home.

Once, Gloria lit a cigarette, took two deep puffs, then pitched the cigarette out the window.

Kate told about the night that Danny Dorman had come to Ray's rooms and—

"Danny, the TV singer?" Gloria interrupted.

"Yes, I was in a Danny Dorman club in high school. Please don't tell anybody it was Danny!"

"I won't. What next?"

Kate told it exactly how it happened, right down to the fifty dollars every week, the scene with her parents, the trip to this place, and how Ray had been so strong in the dark woods.

"That was last night," Gloria said thoughtfully, "when you were still sixteen?"

Kate nodded.

"That's all?"

"Mrs. Wembler did load a gun in her office. She locked me in the bedroom, too, but unlocked the door after Ray had phoned. And she made arrangements for me to meet Ray down the road at six o'clock. Gloria, I'm afraid of him! I don't want him to touch me again! But I have to keep contact with him to save poor Danny Dorman! Gloria, what will I do?"

"Ray Ungas is this rat's real name?"

"Yes."

"Go ahead and meet him, darling," Gloria said cheerfully. "I'll dream up a way to outwit him." Gloria thought a moment, her forehead puckered. "And you still don't understand what this is all about?"

"I'm bewildered."

"I'll make it ABC's, youngster. Danny Dorman is big money, maybe a quarter-million bucks a year from television alone. This Ungas is a greedy nobody, but he did go to grade school with Danny. With a cute doll like you on a string, Ungas manages to get Danny Dorman to his place—and drunk. At the proper time, Ungas lets you out of the closet and you're wearing only a sheer nightgown. What would any normal man, let alone a drunk, do at that moment? So, this Ungas decides the party needs more liquor and out he goes, but my guess is he listened at the keyhole. At the climactic moment, Ungas pops in. He just happens to have a camera lying around and snaps a pic of a TV star and a naked woman—no, a naked sixteen-year-old doll—in the TV star's arms. Sure, it's a game, kid. Blackmail's always a game—a dirty game. If that picture ever got into circulation, Danny Dorman wouldn't last ten minutes in television."

"So," Kate said softly, "he's blackmailing my Danny."

"If you hadn't been so innocent, youngster, you'd have tumbled to the game long ago."

"But why bring me here?" Kate wondered.

Gloria frowned. "Who knew that you and this Ray Ungas were so intimate?"

"No one, I was careful."

"That's why you're here. Ungas is hiding you from Danny Dorman. Or, put it this way. Dorman won't let his vast earnings slip down the drain. Ten to one, Dorman has detectives on Ray Ungas's tail night and day. Those detectives want that picture and they want you. If Ungas told Dorman you're only sixteen or seventeen at the most, Dorman's in a panic. If Ungas is handing you fifty bucks a week, he must be making a mint every month. If those detectives catch up with you, Kate, they can get you on their side and Ungas doesn't want that. He's vulnerable, too, because you're jail-bait. Yes, this Ray Ungas is clever in the way he trapped Dorman and damned dangerous. Ungas has money over a barrel. He'll cut deep into that money and pass on a few bucks to you on a stall that Danny Dorman wants you here. Do you want me to go on?"

"It's clear," Kate said miserably.

"And you must meet Ungas at six o'clock." Gloria laughed. "I'll take care of that, but answer one question. The first time with Ungas—did you like it?"

Kate flushed scarlet.

"All right," Gloria said lightly, "you liked it. What about the second time?"

"I—I—"

"The third time, kid?"

"No!"

"But with the great Danny Dorman?"

"I loved it, every precious second of it!" Kate's lifted face was ecstatic. "I'd do anything that Danny asked. I'd crawl naked in the streets for Danny. He's sweet and kind and tender. I'd bear a child gladly for him."

"Sure, true love—and him drunk. Youngster, stop kidding yourself. If Danny Dorman ever met you, knowing you were the one that night, he'd kick your teeth in. Believe me, Kate, I know his type. To him, you're just as much a threat as Ray Ungas. But, you need help by six o'clock."

Gloria stirred restlessly.

"Youngster, let's make believe that this a military campaign and we must outwit the enemy. A drunken colonel told me there are two objectives in every campaign—the immediate and the long-range. Incidentally, the colonel never made it with me, but he rated the D.S.C. for sustained effort. In fact, only Hector ever crossed my goal line and Hector's going to make it awfully tough for the next man who tries."

Gloria lit a cigarette and smoked thoughtfully.

"I think I've got an answer. According to the colonel, sometimes you by-pass the long-range objective because of the imminence of the immediate. At six o'clock, you're to meet Ray Ungas up the road. Act innocent. You don't know from nothing. We'll win that six o'clock objective and make our long-range plans later."

"But how can we outwit him?"

"Youngster, strip for action!" Gloria stood up with an effort. "Have you ever been an actress?"

"Not really, but—"

"Sure, you played the part of a vitamin in a third-grade play, but who hasn't?" Gloria headed from the bedroom and Kate heard her mutter: "Junior, your mother's busy. Besides, this is May, not the football season."

Quickly, Kate undressed.

CHAPTER SEVEN

WHEN Kate Flick returned to the lonely farmhouse, dusk was settling over the lovely Westchester hills. The air had turned a bit chilly. Kate opened the front door quietly and stepped into the hallway. As if on cue, Mrs. Wembler came forward silently from the direction of her office.

"Oh, it's you, my dear," Mrs. Wembler said affectionately, feigning surprise. "Did you meet with Mr. Adams?"

"Yes."

"And you relayed—ah, my message?"

"About the loaded gun you carry?" Kate smiled innocently. "Oh, I told him all about the nickel-plated gun loaded with six cartridges, that you do not wish him to come here ever, and that you can hit a bull's-eye at thirty yards."

Mrs. Wembler seemed about to burst with suppressed excitement. "What did he say, dear?"

Kate remembered the scene with Mrs. Wembler in the office and how terrified she had been.

"Mr. Adams," Kate said carelessly, "says you must operate a house of cards here. In fact, he laughed at the gun. He said that no woman, even if she had ten machine guns, could equal one man." Mrs. Wembler stiffened, and Kate added: "Mr. Adams sent fifty dollars to you, saying you would understand what it was for. Also, he will phone you in about a week or ten days."

Kate handed the money to Mrs. Wembler, who asked: "Are you leaving immediately with that man?"

"Mr. Adams told me to stay here."

"That is unwelcome news," Mrs. Wembler snapped, turning on her heel and gliding off.

Kate hurried upstairs, tapped on Gloria Marden's door. Gloria said, "Come in," and Kate entered.

Gloria sat relaxed by the window, watching the sunlight ruddy the hill tops.

"You perfect darling!" Kate exclaimed, kissing Gloria impulsively. "I'm so happy I could dance on the roof top!" Kate squirmed and wriggled. "Gosh, I feel like I'm in a strait-jacket. What a schemer you are!"

"I never thought of a strait-jacket to keep you free of Ungas. I take it you had no trouble with him?"

"Not much, thanks to you."

"And you haven't been gone long, less than half an hour." Gloria smiled amusedly. "Did you manage to wangle any information from the blackmailer?"

"Unh, unh. Within ten minutes, Ray seemed in a hurry to drive back to Manhattan, or so he kept saying." Again, Kate wriggled uncomfortably. "He seemed terribly worried or preoccupied, I don't know which. When I asked several guarded questions, I sensed he was only half-listening. Damn him for using that picture to blackmail poor Danny Dorman! If I had had a gun at the car, I'd have—"

"For heaven sakes," Gloria interrupted, "stop wriggling for a few minutes and strip off the clothes, will you?"

A moment later Kate stood undressed. Yards and yards of white gauze were wound about her body, exaggerating her curves, but the wealth of young breasts were bare.

Gloria offered, "No wonder Ungas didn't try to seduce you," and giggled.

Kate began to unwind the gauze strips from her thighs. There were greasy stains on the gauze and Gloria said, "That vaseline I daubed on the bandages looks perfectly horrid. Kate, what did Ungas say?"

"Hah, was he surprised! His face dropped six inches when I told him I had poison ivy!"

"Did he want to—I mean, did he demand proof that you did have the ivy?"

"No, but I presented him with the proof."

Because she had been able to outwit Ungas so easily, Kate's chin lifted proudly. Standing there in the dimness, she seemed much older than seventeen, more poised and sure of her new-found womanly strength since leaving North Street.

"Gloria, I lifted my skirt so he could see the bandages on my thighs. One minute, he was on fire, telling me he had rented a motel for the night—then, all this gauze. He's just terrified by poison ivy! I told him Mrs. Wembler had to call in a doctor, that the doctor said I had the worst case of poison ivy on record." Kate stroked Gloria's face. "You're a wonderful darling! How did you think up the scheme?"

"A girl learns early to protect herself from the predatory male, youngster." Amusement faded from Gloria's face and her eyes hardened. "Poison ivy and bandages is a variation of a much older stratagem. When I used to go out with a man I liked, particularly if there were heavy drinking ahead, I faked my period and that stopped the man or myself, whichever one couldn't be trusted. Tales from an old school, youngster." Gloria shrugged. "Let's get you out of the gauze."

Gloria used scissors on the gauze. Kate wadded the stuff, and crammed it into a waste basket.

"I suppose Mrs. Wembler will put this on my bill," Gloria said dryly. "I used all the gauze in the bathroom."

"I'll pay for the gauze. I doubt that Ray Ungas will try to see me for days. He said he would phone Mrs. Wembler in a week or so, but didn't explain why that was necessary. I asked if there were a police alarm out for me because I ran away from home, but he seemed to think it was too early for that. Do you think that's right, Gloria?"

"Police usually wait forty-eight hours, I think, before sending out an alarm." Gloria dropped the scissors on the vanity. "We're still in the dark as to how Ungas is working the blackmail game, but you can bet that whatever he's planning means no good for someone, maybe Mrs. Wembler. Offhand, I'd reason that Ungas won't come back here unless absolutely necessary. The police take a dim view of blackmailers and Danny Dorman may have a private detective or two on Ungas' tail. Kate, we won the initial skirmish. Let's celebrate victory with a spot of brandy."

Gloria poured, keeping Kate's potion especially light. They drank a toast, success to all women in the messy game with men, and chuckled over the poison ivy trick.

"Damn this confinement," Gloria grumbled. "I feel like a hippo. The doctor ordered plenty of exercise and I walked miles. Lord, what a girl goes through for a moment of carelessness! Anyway, I've only a week left, as the doc promises to give me a shot of something powerful to force child-pains. Youngster, take a lesson from me. Men are on the make. At a brawl, I met a rather famous psychiatrist, who said if I visited his offices he would psychoanalyze me for free. A week later, like the foolish girl I was, I called on him. Sure enough, he asked me to recline on a couch and relax, then he began to pick my brains apart. In about two minutes, I realized he was more interested in probing my body, than my latent psychoses." Gloria laughed good-humoredly.

"Youngster, you're very beautiful in the nude and you make me entirely too envious. Before I turn green with cat-fever, get into some clothes. Oh—and no nudity around Mrs. Wembler."

"What?"

"Skip it."

As Kate dressed, she prattled: "Mrs. Wembler met me downstairs, as if she'd been waiting for my return. She didn't seem happy that I'm staying on. Will she dare lock my door again? Will she try to keep me from you?"

"Her?" Gloria snorted. "The queen can afford to lose money on you, considering the stiff way she charges everyone else. When you stalled Ungas, you did Mrs. Wembler a favor. Kate, don't let her forget that *you* faced Ungas alone, not her. If she dares lock your door, start screaming. And don't let one word slip to her that you're not pregnant. Meanwhile, straighten out your own thinking. If she insists you leave before you're ready, don't hesitate to say that Ungas will come to your aid on the run—and armed with trouble for her. If I know Mrs. Wembler—"

Kate stood at the open window. She heard a step below and peered out. Old Joe stood near the house and Kate beckoned to Gloria, who joined her.

"What's he doing?" Kate whispered.

"Ummm, he's right outside the operating room. Kate, that's the room off Mrs. Wembler's office."

Below them, old Joe squatted by the weatherboards, his face forward. "Don't make a sound," Gloria whispered. "I want to check something."

Gloria rustled from the room. Kate continued to watch. Joe used a knife on the weatherboards. A round piece of wood slipped out. Joe reached in a hand, gently tugged forth a cloth. It was growing darker, which made it difficult for Kate to make out

Joe's actions, but he seemed to be listening at the hole in the wall or peering inside.

Gloria slipped back. "What is he doing?"

Kate told her about the piece of wood and the cloth.

"The Park Avenue doctor's car is here," Gloria hissed. "College girl has a Caesarean tonight. Do you suppose Joe's peeking and—" Gloria broke off the thought. "Youngster, I'm awfully tired and you've had a long day. Mind if I lie down? You go to your room, okay?"

Kate left the window. "Gloria, I don't know how to thank you for all you've done!"

"Forget it. Next time you're near a man, drink two quarts of ice water beforehand and keep your legs crossed all night. I should have followed my own advice, I guess." Gloria shivered. "Steady, Junior. We'll both be out of this in a week." Gloria nudged Kate. "Run along. I'm pooped."

Kate left, wondering why Gloria had become so anxious to get rid of her. Something to do with Joe outside?

The warm sunshine of the late morning brightened Gloria Marden's bedroom. The college girl had had her baby, a girl, and had left for Texas. A full week had passed since Kate had outwitted Ray Ungas with the poison ivy trick. Gloria had kept Kate awfully busy.

Lolling on the bed, Gloria ordered: "One, two, three—straighten!"

Kate poised with arms lifted high.

"So, you want to be a professional model, eh? Touch the toes." Kate lowered. "Dammit, I said touch the toes! One, two, three—and don't take it easy. You need young muscle in the exercises. One, two, three. You must toughen the leg muscles, kid. Harden that stomach. Hold the pose!" Kate touched her toes and waited.

"Up." Kate straightened. "Suck in air, hold it. Let the breasts poke forward, goose. What do you think breasts are for—invisibility?"

Twice a day for hours—and for a week—Gloria had drilled Kate. Clad in nothing but briefs, Kate followed her commands.

"Hit the deck," Gloria ordered.

Kate lay on her back, hands extended over her head, feet close together. Gloria barked an order. Kate lifted and swung her arms forward.

Up and down. Faster, faster. Up and down!

"Hit it hard," Gloria said, stifling a yawn. "What are you, an angel cake?"

After what seemed an hour, Gloria ordered: "Take a rest, youngster. You don't want to be a model, do you?"

"I do!"

Kate closed her eyes and lay still. The first day that Kate had exercised, she had lost four pounds; in one week, she had melted off ten pounds. Gloria had said: "You're overweight. You need muscle to bulwark curves."

The rest period was entirely too short to suit Kate, as Gloria clipped out: "Fetch the books."

Kate rose, found a lightweight book. She inhaled, rose on tiptoes, and set the book carefully on top of her head, keeping the chin level.

Kate posed like a relaxed statue, tempered muscles holding her breasts high, flattening her stomach, all of which accentuated the upper curves.

She began to walk around the room, the book forgotten. She practiced a full turn.

Rock back on one heel, then step forward. As you advance, smile, smile, and glide right into some man's life. You've flesh and blood and bones, but no emotion except to please. Walk, walk, walk. Turn, turn, turn.

"Kate," Gloria had said, "I'm the buyer in from some department store in the sticks. I'm hard-boiled with money to spend. Please me. Smile for me. Keep smiling if I do have a pot-belly—lots of big buyers do! Remember it's the beautiful body inside the nightgown that sells a hundred gowns. Remember. Hey, quarter-turn that breast to me. Point the nipple right at my eyes. Umm, a bit more of the hip curved right at me. And never forget the accentuation of the thrusting breasts. Curves, darling. Never, never angles for the buyer."

Smile.

Force yourself to smile when you really wish to kick in the buyer's teeth!

Think *peaches.* Think *cheese.*

Another thing, kid. Say to yourself: "I'm beautiful, beautiful." Modeling is pure sex, kid.

Quarter-turns from the hips. Peaches. Beautiful. Sex. Cheese. Thrust. Smile.

Over and over again, practice to make it perfect until it jells into an unconscious, beautiful act and fat-bellied buyer from Cedar Rapids drools and thinks: "What's her phone number and what's she doing tonight?" Sell the bastard a hundred-thousand nightgowns. Sell him a billion panty-bra sets. Sell him anything you can wear, but sell him.

Hah, you got him hooked!

"Take a bath," Gloria drawled, "before you drop."

Showing off, Kate mounted the bed, stepped over Gloria's lolling legs to the floor, not once losing the book on her head, not once conscious of the book.

"Smart alec," Gloria jeered.

Kate said, "Yah," and hurled the book into a corner.

In the bathroom, Kate ran the tub half full of hot water and soaked fatigue and aches from tired muscles. It was so delicious, lolling up to the chin, receiving the full benison of hot water.

If she could lie here forever!

"Kate," Gloria called.

"Okay, I'm out of the hot!"

"Yeah? Let's hear the water gurgle."

Water drained from the tub. Kate sat, naked as a new baby, her skin just as pink. She began to run cold water. The cold nipped into her opened pores, puckered the skin on her legs. It was ice, after the heat, shivering from toes up to her spine and into her brain. She slid deeper into the cold water, holding her breath to keep from yelling, and the water lapped over her breasts, the nipples turgid.

Was it worth all this trouble to model?

Yes, yes!

"Kate!"

Time to move.

"Kate, makeup kit."

Kate toweled vigorously, then massaged her face with the heels of her hands until the skin began to glow.

She stepped to the mirror and peered at herself.

Where was the scared teenager who had fled silently from North Street years and years ago?

Kate sensed the change in herself, the acquisition of a maturity far beyond her age and undreamed of a week before. No longer was her face so innocently adolescent. Whatever roundness had been there during life on North Street and at high school had vanished, had been replaced by a soft, lean attraction.

The eyes have not changed, Kate decided dreamily. So wetly velvet, like violet pansies.

Once, she had asked curiously: "What are bedroom eyes, Gloria?"

"An expression men use."

"What do the men mean?"

"That you're meant for a bedroom."

"And?"

"That you're good in a bed."

"To sleep, Gloria?"

"Not to sleep. Bedroom eyes—sexy eyes."

"Gloria, my eyes say I'm good in a bed?"

"I'm not a man."

"My eyes suggest I'm good in a bed with a man?"

"Maybe."

"Don't eyes lie, Gloria?"

"You learn to make your eyes lie to men, youngster. Keep your young heart hard and your eyes a promise."

"I don't want to look sexy! I'm not sexy-looking, am I?"

"You don't resemble an ice cube."

"No, I guess I don't."

"You liked it in bed with Danny Dorman?"

"Yes!"

Kate thought: Your eyes are a promise of love. A young, beautiful promise. Keep your eyes full of promise. Let a man long to kiss you, but be stingy with your kisses. Act easy to get, but be hard to get.

"Kate!" Gloria's voice floated along the hallway. "Did you drown in the tub?"

"Coming!"

"And fetch the makeup kit from your room."

"Right!"

Kate hurried from the bathroom. Without a thought for her nudity, she grabbed the makeup kit from her bedroom and hurried to Gloria for another lesson.

CHAPTER EIGHT

L IKE a warm dream, tender and sweet as only youth can
make it, the May twilight closed around Kate Flick. Clad in
a sweater and light slacks, sandals shodding bare feet, she knelt
beside a bed of Darwin tulips.

"And what is this one named?" she asked eagerly, pointing to
a stately beauty.

Joe, the man who did chores for Mrs. Wembler, said: "It's *Queen
of the Night,* miss." He knelt by Kate. "No tulip is really black, not
even *Tulipe Noire,* which the French developed many years ago." His
elbow brushed against Kate and she turned. His eyes were humor-
ous behind glasses. "Miss, you love everything that is beautiful, eh?"

"Oh yes!"

"Hmmm, I noticed before that you're partial to the most
brilliant colors and pass right over the pastel shades. Deep color
thrills you, eh?"

"It makes me vibrate."

"And you like lots and lots of pretty flowers in your bedroom. But Miss Marden doesn't care for flowers." The old man
shrugged. "It seems like yesterday, sometimes, that I first became
acquainted with tulips."

Every twilight for a week, after Kate had finished with the
lessons and exercises under Gloria Marden's tutelage, she had
joined the old man in the garden. There were several new clients
at the cabins, but Kate stayed away from them, preferring the
company of Gloria or the old man.

And he puzzles me, Kate thought. Obviously, he's very intelligent and well-educated. Why does he work here? And that night at the side of the house—had the old man peered into the operating room or merely listened?

Gloria had advised: "Forget we saw him snooping."

Well, why had he snooped?

Kate said: "Will you tell me about the time you first learned about tulips?"

"That was when I lived in Jersey," Joe began. "A very lovely town, Bernardsville, in the midst of the Somerset Hills, miss. When I was nine years old, my mother gave me some tulip bulbs. I thought they were the ugliest things I'd ever seen, but mother explained that the most beautiful flowers rose from such ugliness. Then, she took a knife and cut one of the bulbs open. Sure enough, right inside she showed me a perfect, tiny flower. Mother said: 'This one won't bloom, of course, but the others will because there is a perfect flower inside them.' I asked: Why did you spoil the bulb?' She said: 'Son, because I wanted you to know the miracle inside. Ugliness often produces beauty. This bulb is like a mother, carrying a baby in her womb, full of life, just waiting its time to be born'."

Joe's eyes sparkled.

"My mother," he explained proudly, "was the finest teacher I ever had and I studied at one of the finest medi—uh, at a very excellent school. Miss, I planted those ugly bulbs. I watched the spot during the long winter. I guess no tulips ever received so much attention. Come spring, and the sprouts pushed into sight, hard and firm, like they could push right up through concrete. The sprouts leaved and fanned out. I watched and watched until one day—"

Someone called out, "Kate!"

Kate looked up. From an upstairs window, Gloria beckoned urgently.

"I'll go to her," Kate said. "Will you tell me the rest of the story later?"

"Yes."

Kate rose.

"Tonight," the old man said, "she has her baby."

"You mean Gloria?"

"Yes. Didn't she tell you?"

"Of course." Curiosity prompted Kate to ask the man, "How did you know about it? Did Gloria tell you?"

The old man glanced at the bed of glistening tulips, gradually losing glorious color in the fast-fading light. He's very sad, Kate thought, and very friendly.

"Miss," he said thoughtfully, "I know about everything on this place and *her*."

"Mrs. Wembler?"

"Her." The old man straightened. "I guess Miss Marden is plenty worried. You tell her not to worry. That doctor she's got isn't very ethical, but he never yet lost a baby here or a mother."

Kate started off.

Joe muttered: "Abortions! That's like my mother cutting that tulip bulb and killing the flower."

Upstairs, Gloria sat on the rumpled bed, her face strained and pale in the soft light from a single lamp. She wore only a nightgown. Her belly was obvious. Kate sat beside her.

"Much pain?"

"I've timed the spasms, they come every five minutes. I'll go down in a few minutes." Gloria shivered. "It's not been any fun, youngster. Believe me, I hope you'll never have to suffer like I have."

"I wouldn't mind. For the right man, Gloria."

"A Danny Dorman?"

"Yes."

"Youngster, someday you'll learn the score about some men. Danny Dorman always thinks of number one, period. Like my Hector, Danny's a rich no-good. Be sensible and stop dreaming about a television singer."

"I love him!" Kate protested.

"Nuts!" Gloria clenched her fingers and winced, holding her breath. "After I have Junior, I'll only need to stay two days. Doc says I can ride with him to New York. Kate, we may never see each other again."

"I'll come see you in New York."

"It might be better if you didn't. You'll only remind me of the few decent days I had in this damn wilderness." Gloria's hand covered one of Kate's. "It's hell that I've gone through for Junior—yet I'll never see him."

Kate stared, wondering if she had heard correctly. "Why won't you see your own baby?" she demanded.

"House rules."

"I don't understand!"

"And who does?"

Gloria's shoulders sagged and Kate wrapped a strong arm about the older woman.

"Youngster, I didn't have to have Junior, but I wanted him. I wanted him for myself even if he were a bastard. Then, I began to do some serious thinking here. A baby should have a good home with loving parents who will take care of him, give him the good start that he needs to become a success. Now, Junior's my baby. He won't be my baby after he's born and I won't ever see him, but Junior's going to have a fine home."

Bewildered, Kate said: "I still don't understand."

"When I came here," Gloria explained, "I signed a paper turning the baby over to Mrs. Wembler."

"She'll keep your baby?"

"Hell, no. She sells the babies immediately."

The words hit Kate like blows. "Gloria, that's the cruelest thing I ever heard!"

"It's fine for the baby. This world is simply no place for a bastard. Any baby deserves the best chance."

"But who would buy a baby?"

"Hundreds of married people who never had babies want babies. It's a damn funny world, youngster. Girls who don't want to become pregnant, like the girls who end up here, are fecund as cats. Married people who long for babies are often sterile. They try and try, but no babies. And they love babies." But suddenly Gloria buried her face against Kate. She sobbed: "Kate, you've got to help me!"

"Anything, darling."

Gloria panted: "I've only a minute or two. They'll take my baby and sell him. I'll never see him, not once. Kate, promise! Find out who adopts him! Find out who the foster parents are!" Gloria's passion was fierce, her tears unashamed, and her arms strong around Kate. "I've got to know the truth. If his parents don't really want him—if they're not the right kind of loving parents—Kate, I'd die!"

"I promise." Kate had not the slightest idea how she would carry out the promise. "Do you feel better, darling?"

"I feel like a slob! Find out who gets Junior, find out where they live!"

"I will."

Someone rapped on the door.

"Yes?" Gloria called out.

Mrs. Wembler said: "He's here, Gloria. I want you downstairs in five minutes."

"All right."

Kate whispered: "Do you think she heard us talking?"

"If she did, she may make your job more difficult. Kate, go to the side of the house. Open that peephole where we saw Joe. You'll be able to hear what they say in the operating room." Tremors shook Gloria's body and she groaned. "Promise?"

"Of course!"

Wearily, Gloria stood up. "Youngster, you're the only person I trust. Bye, now."

"I'll help you downstairs!"

"Not with the queen around." Gloria wiped her tear-stained face. "I'm a sentimental slob." Jauntily, her shoulders squared and she smiled crookedly. "Be seeing you tomorrow and don't worry about me. They say it's easy, like going to sleep. You wake up light-headed and lighter-bellied."

"Gloria!" Kate wailed. "I'm sorry!"

"That's exactly what Hector said." Gloria kissed Kate. "Kid, with a man, keep your legs crossed."

Gloria went out.

Kate sat on the rumpled bed and brooded.

Selling a baby that belonged to someone else, what a terrible way to make money. And an abortion, really killing a baby. Money, money, money! Money made the world go round, didn't it? And what some people would do for money!

Some people?

What about you, Kate Flick?

You never had any money of your own. You sneaked over to Ray Ungas' rooms and you let him have your precious body for a few pretty clothes. Aren't pretty clothes the same as money? You did it for money, not love.

So, what makes you think you're better than the Mrs. Wemblers and a Park Avenue doctor with no ethics?

Actually, Kate Flick, aren't you much worse than they? You sold yourself cheaply, and to a ratty guy who's a blackmailer.

Because of your greed for money, you endangered the career of Danny Dorman.

Was Gloria right about Danny? Was he a no-good with a golden voice?

Not Danny!

Kate glanced at the clock on the night table. Good Lord, Gloria had been gone ten minutes.

In her own bedroom, Kate tugged a dark sweater over the white one she wore and tied a kerchief around her hair. On tiptoes, she slipped into the silent hallway.

At the stairhead, she leaned over the bannister and listened, but there was no sound from downstairs. Of course, no sound. The operating room was sound-proofed, remember? Kate slipped down the stairs and quietly went out the unlocked front door.

Night lay all around, thick and silent. Sound whispered in and roared into engine noise. Headlights tunneled a path along the macadam road.

Ray Ungas in that car?

The car continued on past the farmhouse and the night turned quiet again. Why, Kate wondered, did she think of Ray Ungas? He won't come here.

She stole from the porch and walked the grass to the corner of the house. Here, the sky appeared and distant stars twinkled. A breeze wandered in from the woods and touched her face. Kate trembled and wiped perspiration from her face.

What was it like to have a baby? What was it like to bear a child, but never see the child?

If I have a baby, Kate decided fiercely, nobody will take my baby. If I'm pregnant, I'll keep my baby.

Some people, Gloria had explained, wanted babies, tried to have them, but never succeeded.

Perhaps, Kate thought, I'm sterile. No matter how many times I perform the sex act, I'll never bear a child. Maybe I'm lucky.

Lucky never to become pregnant?

Kate advanced cautiously along the run of the sidewall, relieved to notice that there were no lights on this side, not even in the room where Ray Ungas had threatened Mrs. Wembler so long ago. Glancing upward, she located Gloria's bedroom.

Now—from up there, they had spotted old Joe below, not directly below them, but several paces toward the rear. How far along the wall?

The house rested on a solid concrete foundation which was two feet above ground level. Again, Kate studied the position of Gloria's bedroom window. Right about here, she decided, and touched the weatherboards.

Find that peephole, she thought. Already, Gloria may have had her baby and you won't be able to hear them talking inside.

How long does it take for a baby to be born?

The weatherboards were smooth and cold to her touch. In which one would the peephole be? Not the lowest one, probably. The next board up? Kate tested that board with her fingers. How could she find the peephole?

Anxiety guided her fingers.

Push against the board, you fool! Why didn't you bring a flashlight?

She worked along the length of the board and glanced up. She had advanced too far beyond the bedroom window and retraced her steps. That peephole had to be here, but where?

She knelt on the ground. She pressed nervous fingers against the third weatherboard from the foundation, intent on the task, worried by the passage of time. Suddenly, she froze. Panic coursed up her spine and exploded inside her brain.

There! Shoes on the ground! She stared at the feet, unable to move. Pants legs above the shoes.

I'm caught! she moaned inwardly.

A man whispered, "It's all right," and Kate looked up.

Noiselessly in the night, old Joe had joined her. He patted Kate's shoulder and his touch was friendly.

"What are you doing, miss?"

"Nothing!"

"Trying to find a hole in the wall, eh?"

"Yes!"

"I'm no fool." He chuckled. "She might look here, you know. I don't take chances. I've outsmarted her."

"How?" Kate panted.

He countered: "Why is it necessary for you to come here?"

Kate hesitated.

"You can trust me, miss."

"Please help me," Kate pleaded softly. "Gloria's worried. She wants her baby to have a fine home and she wants me to find out who the foster parents are."

"Did you see me once at the side of this house?"

"Yes! Please hurry!"

"There's no point to hurrying, ever," he drawled. "I check on her all the time. Sure, I've got a peephole into the operating room, miss. To hear, not to see. You could press against those board for hours, but you'd never find the cut-out section. There are two layers of boards and I cut at an angle so the section won't press in. And the putty around the section matches the siding perfectly so she can't find my peephole. Inside the operating room, behind a cabinet, I have another section and that pulls into the space between the studs. I can hear anything they say by listening from here." He patted Kate's shoulder. "You come with me."

"I must find out who will get Gloria's baby!"

"No need for you to wait, miss."

"I promised Gloria!"

"Hush, you come with me." He urged Kate to her feet, and she stood a half-head taller than the old man. "I know who will get her baby."

"And you'll tell me?"

"Later. You see, Miss Marden isn't the first one to come here and worry about the foster home for her baby. So, I learn everything that goes on around here. You come with me, miss. Can't tell who might come along, maybe *her*."

Kate followed him, knowing that he hated Mrs. Wembler. When they approached the graveled driveway at the rear, he stayed on the lawn, the grass muffling their steps. They entered the barn-garage through a sidedoor where Mrs. Wembler's new station wagon was parked.

"The doctor," Joe said, "always parks east of the house on a woods lane that belongs to Mrs. Wembler. He uses a path through the woods to reach the house unnoticed. He sure is a cautious man, that high-priced doctor, but he knows the female body like he knows his hands. Don't worry about that doctor. He's itchy-fingered, but a top operator."

Taking Kate's hand, he led her to a set of stairs and up the stairs to a door which he opened. "Inside," he said, and Kate went in. The door closed. A switch clicked.

Soft light from a shaded lamp pooled on a thin rug. There were two windows in the room, each covered with thick, cheap drapes. The walls were of knotty pine with several recessed book-cases filled with scores of books.

"I came here eight years ago, answering an ad for an elderly handman," he explained. "I fixed up this room like it is now." He gestured to a single maple bed with a green spread. "I bought that. She won't spend a dime unless it's on herself. Sit down, Miss Flick."

Kate sat on the edge of a club chair that had seen better days and waited.

"Do you trust me, miss?"

Kate nodded.

"And I trust you. This is a queer setup. I've thought a lot about it since I came here. Maybe I'm too philosophical. Young girls are bound to get themselves into all kinds of mischief, no matter how careful they are. To help them, there must be certain doctors with a Mrs. Wembler somewhere in the background. At a stiff fee, of course. Mind if I smoke, Kate?"

"No."

Joe loaded a blackened brier pipe, lit up, and puffed contentedly as he wandered around the small room.

"This is a gold mine, miss. The fact is they'd rather the girls had their babies and not abortions. That's good business because they sell a baby for fifteen-hundred dollars or more, depending on how badly people want a baby."

Joe faced Kate.

"You tell Miss Marden not to worry about the foster parents of her baby. They are—" He paused, regarding Kate thoughtfully. "Right now, you're too upset for me to tell you the foster parents' name. You like Miss Marden and she'll be upset right after the baby comes. You'd tell her who the people are and the chances are she'd rush right over there. If she made a scene, that would be bad for this place and for me, miss. Let's wait a day or so until Miss Marden calms down and gets adjusted to the loss of her baby. Then, you can sneak over and see the parents. Even if you don't like the foster parents, you mustn't tell that to Miss Marden. Promise?"

What he had said made sense to Kate and she promised.

"Miss, what do you think of me?"

"I like you."

"Generally, the girls do, but not the snooty kind. Are you planning to have your baby, eh?"

"I'm not pregnant." The words had slipped from Kate's tongue before she could censor them. "I didn't mean to tell that!"

He smiled around the pipe. "Of course, you didn't." Smoke curled around his face. "I knew it anyway."

"What?"

"I knew it already."

"But how?"

"Don't think me a snoop, please. Sometimes when Mrs. Wembler was away, you and Miss Marden talked too loud. Knowing what goes on here is a form of insurance with me. I'm old. I want a warm place to live when I'm too old to work. So, I must have a real hold on her. How long will you stay here, Kate?"

"I'm not sure."

"Will this Ray Ungas take you away?"

That he knew Ray's name seemed natural, now.

"I don't know."

"He's no good for you, miss. When you leave, what do you plan to do?"

"I'm not sure."

"Go home?"

"Never!"

Joe laid the pipe down. "You wait here. And don't worry about your friend." At the door, Joe turned. "I've got to check on things. You should know one thing, Kate. You're the only one I've ever let come up here. You see, I trust you."

"Thank you."

"And look around."

He went out and closed the door.

A strange old man, Kate thought. He hates Mrs. Wembler, but he continues to work for her. Insuring himself of a warm place later. Blackmail? No!

The books drew her to the shelves. Idly, she read the names of the authors. Shakespeare, Savonarola, Goethe, Wesley, Proust, Plato, and a dozen others, but only Shakespeare was familiar. There were books on gardening and flowers, and four much-thumbed volumes on bulbs. Kate noticed several thick books.

Genetics. Bio-chemistry. Theory of Medicine.

Why such books here?

She opened one volume. On the flyleaf in faded script she saw: Joseph M. Cramer, Sept. 1909, HMS.

That name must belong to the old man.

Kate remembered that once he had told her he was seventy-one years old. In 1909—she calculated swiftly—why, in 1909, he had been twenty-one years old.

At twenty-one, where had be been?

HMS.

For some title or—wait, HMS were the initials of "His Majesty's Ship."

Medical books on some British ship?

She returned the book to the shelf and selected one of the bulb books. Sitting on the easy chair, she thumbed the pages, studying the colored plates and admiring tulips, daffodils, and lesser bulbs, heralds of spring. She turned back to chapter one, "Origin of Dutch Bulbs," and began to read.

Time passed and the book engrossed her. She was well into the second chapter when a light step sounded on the stairs and she arose. The old man entered.

"A baby girl," he said, and smiled. "Seven pounds, nine ounces. A fine girl, healthy. You should have heard that baby cry, miss. Tell Miss Marden not to worry."

A lump formed in Kate's throat. "I'm so glad! Though she always called her baby, junior! Gloria's all right?"

"Of course." He crossed to Kate and read the book title. "A good book, Kate. Did you like it?"

"It's fascinating. I'm so happy that the baby is a girl! And Gloria's all right?"

"Yes. Take the book with you. It's late and I've a long day ahead. Goodnight, Kate."

At the door, Kate remembered something that had puzzled her. She asked frankly: "What does HMS mean?"

The question did not startle him. He stood quietly. Gradually, the expression on his face changed and Kate thought: He's not here, but miles and miles away. Back in 1909?

The old man murmured, "Harvard Medical School," and Kate opened the door and crept down the stairs.

CHAPTER NINE

JUNE warmed the Westchester hills.

Pensively, Kate Flick sat by an open bedroom window and watched the sun gild the woods and fields, the bed where tulips had bloomed and died. Lunch was an hour distant, and ten rapid days had passed since Gloria's baby daughter had been born. The days had been filled.

From old Joe, the handyman who had studied at Harvard Medical School, Kate had learned the name of the foster parents of Gloria's illegitimate baby. When Gloria had seemed resigned to the loss of the daughter, Kate had left the farmhouse early, walked the macadam road to the Parkway, then hitchhiked a ride to Yonkers. Posing as an unemployed maid who had been sent to the Borzen home by a non-existent employment agency in New York City, Kate had been able to gain entrance to the house and talk to Mrs. Borzen.

The Borzen home was middle-class, in excellent taste. Mr. Borzen, she learned, owned a small store in Yonkers, a Buick sedan, and seemed in comfortable circumstances. Although they had been married for a dozen years, they had had no children. Mrs. Borzen was a pleasant woman in the middle-thirties, deeply in love with the infant daughter.

"Isn't she a perfect darling?" she had asked Kate. "Oh, we're so happy! We thought we'd never have a child, then a miracle happened and I became pregnant. The last month, I stayed at my mother's, she lives upstate.

Kate had agreed that the baby was indeed a darling, keeping to herself the knowledge that the baby had been adopted. She had understood the reason for Mrs. Borzen not staying in Yonkers the "last month", thus neighbors would not know that the infant was not hers by legitimate birth.

"And she looks exactly like me," Mrs. Borzen had cooed, cradling the infant.

Kate had agreed, "Just like you," but had noted that the infant seemed to favor Gloria Marden about the eyes.

Satisfied that the deception would succeed and that the infant was in the best of hands, Kate had prepared to go.

"I'm sorry you made the fruitless trip from New York," Mrs. Borzen had apologized. "I don't know where the employment agency obtained my name, because we do not plan to have a maid."

"Perhaps," Kate had suggested, "they read the announcement of the birth in the newspaper and simply sent me here on the chance you might offer me a job. I'll certainly give them a piece of my mind when I return."

"They had a nerve!" Mrs. Borzen had agreed. "Why, I wouldn't let any stranger even touch my baby, not after the hard time I went through to get her!"

Kate had left, pleased with Mrs. Borzen. I suppose, she had thought, people will go to any lengths to obtain a baby if they really love children. They'll even pay a Mrs. Wembler fifteen hundred dollars.

Gloria had accepted Kate's report and added: "Youngster, don't ever tell me who the foster parents are. If I crawl to you, don't tell me. I'd only go to Yonkers and make a nuisance of myself. I'll miss her. Lord, how I'll miss her!"

The next morning, Kate had discovered that Gloria Marden had left the farmhouse sometime during the night, not even bothering to leave a farewell note or a forwarding address.

I suppose it's best that way, Kate had reasoned. Every time I phoned or wrote Gloria, it would only remind her of this place and her daughter. Better that the rope be cut. Obviously, she wants it that way.

Except for her acquaintance with old Joe Cramer, Harvard Medical School, 1909, Kate made no attempt to meet any of the new clients. She avoided Mrs. Wembler, also, and as the days had passed there had developed a sort of armed truce between them.

She spent much time with the old man and wondered about him, although he never opened up again to her.

What were the missing links in his life? Had he graduated and become a doctor? What had happened to reduce him to the level of a handyman, to burying the garbage for a woman he hated?

Always, since leaving North Street, nothing but mysteries. Ray Ungas, with whom she had little contact. Danny Dorman, and nothing of him. Gloria Marden and her Hector, the rich no-good. And the girls who came here shyly, then vanished silently. And Mrs. Wembler, whom Gloria had called a "queen", of whom she had warned: "Don't ever let her see you in the nude." Then the mystery of the old man who had studied medicine at Harvard.

Downstairs, the phone rang. Kate remembered that Mrs. Wembler had driven off to shop, so she hurried downstairs and answered the phone.

"Kate Flick," a familiar voice said. "She there?"

"This is Kate."

His voice lowered to a guarded whisper: "Look, this is important. Walk along the road toward the parkway, understand? In fifteen minutes."

"But—"

"Fifteen minutes on the dot."

Ray hung up. Fifteen minutes and another meeting with that repulsive blackmailer. Kate shrugged, confident that she would not have sex trouble with him today.

Thank God, she thought, I'm not pregnant, for sure. Right in the midst of my period. Did that mean she was sterile, never could have a baby? Maybe it meant that Ray was sterile, the rat! And what did he want today?

Kate strolled the road, loitered by a fence in the midst of woods, and listened to bird songs. A curious gray squirrel scolded from a nearby red oak, then scampered off on its own business. A panel truck went past, lettered NORDEN'S GROCERY, MT. KISCO on the side. Ray Ungas was prompt.

He arrived at the wheel of a new Cadillac, one elbow draped negligently on the door. The profits of blackmail, Kate thought. Then Ray spotted her and braked.

"You look good," he offered grandly. "Get in."

Kate joined him on the front seat.

Turning the car around, he drove toward the Parkway and then to the familiar woods lane. His hair was freshly clipped, crew-cut style, and redolent with tonic. A natty scarf was tied around his scrawny neck, the ends tucked inside the front of a gaudy sports jacket. He wore expensive tan slacks, brown socks with white clocks, and brown-white shoes. His fingernails were clean and neatly trimmed, but Kate noted that his jauntiness seemed forced as if he were unsure of himself.

"Like the heap?" Ray asked, cutting the switch.

"Very nice. How could you afford it?"

"That new job in Manhattan pays me a bundle of cash. Oh, let's not forget you." Ray pulled a roll of bills carelessly from a jacket pocket, counted out five twenties and laid them in Kate's cold hands. "Danny Dorman don't never forget! He sent this. Yeah, from dear old Danny!"

"Why?"

"Danny likes you. He's got a memory."

"Did he send any message?"

"Well, no. Just to sit tight. He's got a wife, remember? The guy's got to be careful." Ray slid across the seat, draped an arm possessively around Kate's shoulders. "Jeez, you sure fill out a sweater good. And I missed you, kid."

Kate waited, knowing what to expect next, and Ray didn't disappoint her. One hand slid under the hem of the green skirt that Gloria had given her.

"Ray."

"Yeah?"

"I'm not pregnant."

"That's good news."

"Ray, I've the proof."

Ray stared, not comprehending at first. "You're in the middle of—" He growled to a stop.

"Yes."

"An' I hotfooted up from Manhattan for nothin'?"

"Yes."

He eyed her suspiciously. "This another stall?"

"For heaven's sake, check if you don't believe me!" Kate forced herself to turn on the seat and face him. "I don't ever keep a secret from you. You keep secrets from me, don't you?"

"Well—"

"If we're together, partners in this game, why don't you tell me more about it?"

Ray pulled her close, kissed her wetly. Kate relaxed, not enjoying the kiss, but playing along, hoping to put him in a better mood.

Ray grumbled: "I'm always outa luck with you."

"In a few days, you won't be disappointed."

"We'll go to a motel."

"All right." Kate pressed her breasts hard against him, nuzzled his shaved face. "Ray."

"Yeah?"

"Tell me more about this game with Danny Dorman, why he pays me the money."

"You don't understand about games."

Kate snuggled closer, playing her own game. "I'm a big girl, darling. I grew up in a hurry since leaving North Street." Her hair touched his chin and she stroked his face. "You said we're partners. You said we'd become rich. I'm not rich—yet. I want more money, darling. Tell me about the game, partner."

"We'll be getting plenty, kid."

"How?"

"From Danny Dorman. And from Mrs. Wembler, see?"

"But I don't see, darling." Kate slid a hand past the scarf and let the hand lay against Ray's undershirt. "Don't hold out on me, please! I want to know how we're going to get money from Danny and Mrs. Wembler."

"Well—" For a moment he hesitated. "Look, with Danny it's the picture."

"The one you took that night at your place?"

"Yeah. Danny don't want nobody to see that pic. Jeez, there he sits on a throne, earnin' a quarter-million bucks a year from TV an' me only drivin' a delivery truck."

Kate lifted her face and opened her eyes wide. She made her eyes moistly beautiful, as she had practiced before the mirror—promise in her eyes and hate in her heart.

"Danny pays us because of the picture, darling?"

"Yeah."

"If we could get more pictures like that—"

"One's enough with Danny."

"Ray, let me see the picture!"

Ray wriggled uncomfortably. "This is a man's game. I mailed one print to Danny, the only one I got developed."

"What about the negative? Make me a print!"

"I can't."

"Why not?"

Ray hesitated. Kate rubbed her breasts across his jacket and kissed the point of his chin lightly.

"Ray! I can hardly wait till next week and the motel!"

"Jeez, you're a hot number."

"For you—next week. Where's the negative?"

"In a bank. Safe in a tin box."

Tenderly, Kate kissed Ray on the lips. "You're no fool, darling. I don't want to be one, either. I want minks and cars and everything expensive." She leaned back from the hips, quarter-turning her breasts, one nipple outlined under the tight sweater and pointed right at him. "How do we tap Mrs. Wembler?"

"She's a push-over. You want more than fifty bucks a week?"

"I want a thousand!" Kate knew enough about the Wembler setup to guess how Ray would move in on the woman. "I've been thinking—about us, darling. The other girls who come to her place have money and always a rich man in the background. Know what? I jotted down their names! Once, I saw a man at one of the cabins. It was night, so I slipped into the nearby woods where they always park and I wrote down the license number. Ray! He's rich and married, a big wheel in advertising. Ray, that car was a Jaguar."

Ray practically drooled. "You sure."

"Of course I'm sure." Kate pouted prettily. "I'm going to find out more about this rich man. The girl likes to talk. Umm, she'll be at Mrs. Wembler's for a month so we don't have to hurry this." Kate's eyes were guilelessly violet "See what a good partner I am?"

"Right. Me, I know how to make the touch, chill 'em off like I done to Danny." His face clouded. "An' that's rough. He's got a coupla detectives around, but they don't scare me. You keep playing right with me. Get the names, more license numbers."

"Partners."

"Sealed with a kiss, kid."

They kissed, long and heatedly, then Kate pushed gently from Ray. "Next week, darling," she murmured.

"Damn right!"

"I'd better go back now."

"Why?"

"Mrs. Wembler's in town shopping. She lost her cook and she has to do all the cooking, which she hates. And I don't want her to suspect that I met you and we laid plans to take her for plenty. Ray, she must be awfully rich!"

"We'll take her, but good." Ray sat silent for a moment, his eyes greedy. "Yeah, you scat back to the house. You get more names, all the dope, see?"

"Ray! Did I ever tell you how wonderful you are?"

"Huh?"

"Ray, you're wonderful!"

Kate ran lightly to the macadam road, waved to Ray, then turned toward the farmhouse. Behind her, the Caddy backed from the woods and tooled off.

Kate walked swiftly, her face on fire. When she reached a brook that ran under the road, she went down the bank and the bridge hid her from the sight of anyone passing.

Wetting a handkerchief, she wiped her lips. She muttered, "He's a rat," and rewet the handkerchief, sponging her face savagely. "Not once did he suspect what I was up to!" She washed her hands. "What a greedy sap he is!" Lifting her skirt and slip, she washed her thigh where his moist hand had touched her. "He won't blackmail much longer. I'll make sure of that—even if I have to kill him!" Kill him?

Delicious idea!

Kill him a hundred different ways, make him suffer the way he had made others suffer.

She mounted the bank and walked toward the farmhouse, thinking of what she must do to outwit Ray Ungas. He must never be allowed to blackmail the girls who came to Mrs. Wembler's place. By the time Kate had reached the farmhouse, she had arrived at a very important decision.

Two points in a military campaign, Gloria had said. The immediate objective and the long-range plan.

Mrs. Wembler had not yet returned. It was time to set in motion the long-range plan. Kate dialed a number at the phone. A woman answered politely.

Kate said: "Mr. Perron, please."

"And why do you wish to talk to him?"

"Tell him one word, *Ray.*"

"I don't understand. Who are you, please?"

"You don't have to understand. Give him the message."

A long pause, then a man said over the phone: "This is Perron. What's with Ray?"

"You are D. D.'s agent, aren't you?"

"Look here, miss! Who are you and—"

"I'm the girl," Kate interrupted.

"What girl?"

"Violet-eyes. Newark. In February, Mr. Perron."

There sounded a whoosh of released breath at the other end of the line. "I want to get in touch with you—fast. Uh—Danny wants to meet you again."

"Can you pick me up?"

"Sure. Where?"

"Five P.M. Mt. Kisco."

"Where in Kisco, violet-eyes?"

"Ummm, bus terminal."

"And how do I make you, darling?"

"You don't," Kate purred. "White sweater, green skirt, green pocketbook."

"A dozen girls may look like that and—"

Kate interrupted, "Not with violet eyes," and broke the connection.

Upstairs, she thought: That's the way to outwit Ungas, go right to dear Danny and tell him everything. And thanks to Gloria, who knew Perron was Danny's agent. Danny will love you more for going straight to him.

She could hardly wait. Lord, five o'clock at Mt. Kisco. Did Kisco have a bus terminal?

It better have one!

Dear Danny Dorman!

CHAPTER TEN

THE LEAN man in the 1953 Ford coupe drove carefully, both hands attentive on the wheel. Somewhere on the parkway north of Yonkers, he had swung west, driving slowly. Under the rim of a felt hat, his hair was black, slightly salted. He had dark eyes and a too-fat bulge under his chin, but he was still lean-looking in a blue shirt with darker blue tie, gray conservative suit, and black shoes.

Why, Kate wondered, doesn't he talk?

Kate stirred restlessly. "Much further?" she asked.

"No," said Mr. Perron.

"And we're really going to Danny?"

"To Danny."

He stared straight ahead, his eyes darker in the gathering twilight and his face expressionless.

An ancient man, Kate thought. Maybe forty.

The good road wound between wooded hills. Here and there, lights were on in houses set well back from the road. They met few cars on the road. The Ford braked, the driver cut the wheels, and the car slid between stone pillars banked with masses of impenetrable evergreens. Gravel crunched under the wheels. The driveway curled through a stretch of lawn spotted with huge trees and stopped before a stone house with many leaded windows and a slate roof. Front lights were on at the entrance, but the rest of the house lay in darkness.

"Danny's place?" Kate asked, overwhelmed by the magnificence of the estate.

"Not exactly, but don't worry. Danny's here."

The lean man got out, rounded the car, and opened the door politely. He helped Kate to the ground. He offered, "Inside," and fingered Kate's elbow gently, urging her to the front door.

The door was unlocked and he opened it. "Go right inside, Danny's expecting you. And I'll drive you back." Kate entered and the door closed at her back.

Kate's heart pounded in excitement. Her cheeks flushed and she seemed about to suffocate.

She stood in a wide vestibule, the floor of flat, polished flagstones. An inner door stood invitingly open. She moved into a wide, high-vaulted hallway. The walls were of fumed oak; sedate, wooden, high-backed chairs were spotted here and there; and the rug was thick and deep underfoot so that she almost tripped as she advanced.

Walk like a model; she thought. Keep the chin high and walk with poised grace and—

A man emerged from an arched doorway to the right. Kate's breath stopped. He was about her own height, maybe an inch or two taller. His hair was blond and curly, one lock loose over a wide forehead. His face was lean, the cheekbones high and prominent; his eyes were familiarly blue and his lips were parted in a boyish grin.

Kate stopped breathing.

He said, "Long time no see." His voice was soft and reassuring, like a whisper caressing velvet. Frankly, his eyes appraised Kate. "You were beautiful that night, but you've changed. Even more beautiful."

"Thank you," Kate said happily.

"And you'll never know, my dear, how much money I spent to find you and didn't."

"I thought Ray told you—Danny, he could have told you where I was!"

"My old pal from grade school. The stingy louse wanted to keep you for himself, I suppose." Danny fingered Kate's arm and she shivered. "Cold?"

"Oh, no."

"Worried?"

"No."

"Not afraid of me?"

"No!"

"What's the matter?"

"Danny, I waited weeks, and weeks for this!"

"This?"

"Meeting you again!"

"I've been around." Danny seemed amused. "Shall we go inside and talk, my dear?"

"Yes, I've so much to tell you."

They went into the room from which Danny had emerged. Kate thought it romantically dim with a huge fireplace at one end, lush drapes at the windows, inviting furniture, and another deep rug, but her eyes were all for Danny.

"Over here," Danny said, and led her to a divan.

Danny slouched on the cushions, relaxed. Kate sat tensely on the cushion edge.

"You are so young and beautiful," Danny murmured. "And lovely violet eyes. Why did you run way from me?"

"I ran?"

"We couldn't find you."

"I had trouble at home, Danny. It was Ray's idea to take me to Westchester. He should have told you."

Danny said quietly: "I don't even know your name."

"It's Kate."

"A strong name. The rest?"

"Flick."

"Come, you can do better than that," Danny chided. "What's your real name?"

"It is Flick."

"Did you ever think of a stage career, Kate?"

"No, but I'd like to model. I've worked hard to train myself. I don't mind the hard work."

"Maybe I can help you, Kate. I've connections." He leaned forward. "Would you like to help me, Kate?"

"Yes."

He patted her hand. "How old are you, Kate?"

"Twenty—no, that's not the truth! I'm seventeen."

"When was your last birthday, Kate?"

"In May."

Danny's face was thoughtful. "We met in February, I remember. And you were sweet sixteen?"

Danny kissed her lightly on the lips and settled back on the cushions, his fingers working nervously. "Why did you wish to see me, Kate?"

"Because I found out what Ray was doing to you."

"My old pal! Youngster, he took me good. Oh—you know that he blackmailed me?"

"Yes. He told me today. That's why I came."

"Kate."

"Yes?"

"You're a big girl and very nice. Unfortunately, I'm married. You know that?"

Kate nodded.

"Frankly, Ray has been difficult. Why don't you tell me your side of the story, right from the beginning, okay?"

"All right."

"Sit back and relax. We're alone. I won't tell you the hell I've gone through because of Ray Ungas and that one night." He seemed sad, more like a boy than a famous man. "I suppose when a guy hits the top of the ladder everybody comes around for a chunk of the money he makes." Danny's voice was soft and sad. "Tell me everything, darling."

And Kate told him. Right from that first meeting with Ray Ungas at the corner candy store. Three times with Ray, but passing lightly over that, stressing the need for money, all about her father and mother and the poverty, the Bible reading on North Street. Then, unexpectedly the delicious meeting with her idol.

Danny listened intently. Once he said: "I missed that bit, darling. Just a little louder, please."

How she had run from home to Westchester and about Mrs. Wembler and the unfortunate girls, how she had worried about pregnancy.

"You're not pregnant?" Danny asked incredulously.

"No, thank God!"

Kate finished with the events of the day, how she had tricked Ray Ungas with kisses and promises so that he told all about blackmail, and his plans to blackmail Mrs. Wembler and the girls who were her clients.

"Danny dear," Kate said, "I'm sorry for all the trouble Ray gave you. If I had known for a moment what he was up to, I'd have come to you sooner."

"One question, darling. Did you know I would be at Ray's rooms that night in February?"

"No."

"I'd gone to Newark for a personal appearance, Kate. Ray met me afterward and we had a couple of drinks. You know, old times in the back alleys. I didn't want to be snooty with him and went up to his home. You expect me to believe that a beautiful, talented girl like you actually fell for a crumb like Ray Ungas?"

Kate blushed furiously. "I was young and a fool."

"What did you see in him?"

"I—I don't know. Maybe I was lonely."

"And you've told the whole story, Kate?"

"Yes."

Danny said loudly: "Okay, okay."

Lights blazed in the room and Kate blinked. Two men entered. One was the lean man who had driven the car; the other was older and chunkier, almost bald, coatless and perspiring, and his shirt sleeves rolled up.

"You get it?" Danny asked, his voice crisp.

"Sure," the old man grunted. "She should write novels."

"Bad novels," Danny agreed. "Cripes, the only reason she went to that crumb was to cut in on the cash."

The bald man said, "Sure," and the lean man nodded.

Danny stood up. "Kate," he said.

"Yes?"

"It's all on tape, every little word we said in here. Know what that means?"

"No."

"You're a beautiful liar trying to get off the hook. You know damn well we're closing in on Ungas and you want out. That's why you came here." His voice was hard, the words clipped off. "You keep your mouth shut about me. You open your mouth and I take that tape to the police. First, you get your teeth kicked in and I mean kicked in!"

"Danny, I told you the truth!"

He called her a filthy name. "Stand up!"

Bewildered, Kate stood. She could not believe the change she saw in Danny Dorman, her idol. His face was a mask, jerking spasmodically. His blue eyes were cruel and deadly. Could this be the real Danny Dorman?

Why, Kate thought, he looks like Ray Ungas!

"You dirty liar, trying to get off the hook!"

Danny's voice was strident and nasty. He spewed names at Kate, gutter language, filth that she had seen scribbled on walls and back fences, horrible names and every one for her. On and on he ranted, beside himself, poisoning the room with his filthy tongue. With no warning, he slapped Kate, just as hard as Ray Ungas had slapped. In the quiet room, the slap sounded like a shot and he laughed, proud of what he had done.

Kate cringed. Danny slapped her again.

Kate's eyes blazed. The new strengths that she had developed since leaving North Street flowed through her body. She faced him, alone and unafraid.

"Underneath," she said scornfully, "you're no different from Ray Ungas. You both prowled the back alleys and learned filth together. No wonder Ray scared you with a threat. You're a rat and rats scare easily. Go back to TV where you'll be safe. Charm the foolish females, but don't let them get close to you or your filth will rub off."

Danny cried out like an animal. He doubled a fist and swung wildly at Kate. She stepped aside and waited. If he tried to strike her again she would take off one shoe and beat him with the heel.

Danny moved in, but the lean man in the gray suit stepped forward and wrapped an arm around Danny. "You hit her where it shows," he warned. "You want her chilled and I'll belt her. Knock it off, Danny."

"She hit me!" Danny ranted, frothing at the mouth.

The lean man repeated, "Knock it off," and wrestled Danny across the room.

"If you bastards were any good," Danny bleated, "you'd have stopped them long ago!"

"Sure. But you didn't want any scandal, remember?"

The lean man closed a door and walked to Kate. "The guy's been through a lot because of you an' he can't take it. I told him I'd do the belting. If you try another bite on him, you'll need surgery, sister."

Kate wanted to collapse on the divan and sob. Her face burned from the stinging slaps, but she stood proudly, chin lifted, eyes wide and alive, and chest upthrust as she breathed raggedly. But she was glad she had come here and learned what Danny was.

"And I organized a fan club for him," Kate snapped. "To think I once drooled over him. He's a sewer rat with the gilt of TV hiding his commonness. For a half hour every week—"

The lean man interrupted: "Knock it off, sister, or I'll belt you one."

Kate laughed. "Danny Dorman scares easily," she jeered, but her heart was full of misery. "Maybe you scare, too."

She walked around the lean man, moving in the proud, graceful manner that Gloria Marden had taught her, putting on a brave show, her legs all the while ready to buckle. She thought *cheese,* and forced a gay smile. She walked into the hall-way, out to the waiting Ford, the lean man tagging along.

He grumbled: "I'm supposed to drive you back."

"How awfully considerate of you, working for pay." Kate knew she had gained an advantage over him. Yes, and an advantage over Danny Dorman. Reverse the positions of Danny and Ray, and it would have been Danny who had put the bite on Ray. Kate ordered: "Open the door, please."

He opened the door and Kate sat down. He slammed the door. Rounding the Ford, he opened the far door, slid under the wheel, and slammed the door shut.

"Feel better?" Kate mocked.

"Look, I don't like this work sometimes. A guy has to eat and the job pays well. Crumbs like Danny Dorman, who don't know any better than to shack up with jail-bait, have to be protected. Not always from others, but from themselves. I know Danny. When he's drunk, he's on the make, and when he's not drunk, that's news. A rich no-good, that's Danny Dorman. Like I said, it's a job I do and—"

Kate echoed him bitterly, "Knock it off," and the car gunned off, the rear tires spitting gravel carelessly.

Twice, the lean man started to make conversation, but Kate remained aloof. Near Mrs. Wembler's place, she did say: "I'll walk the rest of the way alone."

"You keep your pretty nose clean," the lean man grumbled. "You come at Danny again and you get belted, but good. He's got movie stars on his string and you're jail-bait, sister. You want to lose teeth, just come at Danny again."

Kate said quietly, "You didn't keep Ray Ungas off Danny Dorman, but I can," and the lean man swore.

Kate stepped out and the car shot forward.

When the Ford had disappeared, Kate lost her composure. She stumbled into the woods, fell flat, and buried her face in the dead leaves. Sobs racked her body. Her fingers dug into the dirt.

End of a dream, she thought. Now you know how Gloria felt that night you saw her crying alone.

Overhead, the stars shone down, distant and remote, as unsympathetic as the nearby trees.

CHAPTER ELEVEN

SOMEONE, possibly one of Danny Dorman's detectives, had tipped off Mrs. Wembler to the blackmail play that Ray Ungas planned for her and the clients. The next morning, she summoned Kate to the sound-proofed office.

"I don't know what to do, nor where to turn," Mrs. Wembler said, studying Kate carefully. "Will you help me?"

Kate shrugged. She had slept very little during the night, but now she was cold and calm, having gained strength from the encounter with Danny Dorman.

"My dear! You must enjoy some hold over your Mr. Adams—ah, Ray Ungas is his real name, I've been told." Mrs. Wembler leaned across the desk. "Do you hate Ungas?"

Kate waited, ignoring the question.

"If that man tries to blackmail my clients, think of the misery he will cause! Think what he can do to Gloria Marden!"

"I'm thinking," Kate said carefully, "of the babies whom you sold so callously."

"It was the only way for them, my dear."

"Really?"

"Only the best people obtain my babies." A vein jumped on Mrs. Wembler's neck. "What do you plan to do about Ungas?"

"I suppose," Kate mused, "there must be some place like this for the girls to go—at a stiff price."

There was no point in jabbing needles into Mrs. Wembler further, so Kate said: "I walked into this setup innocently and blindly. I don't care whether or not you believe that, but Gloria Marden did. I'm not one bit interested in you, Mrs. Wembler, or whether anyone blackmails you. I've decided what I shall do and I'm going through with it to help Gloria and the others. The revolver, please."

"Eh?"

"The nickel-plated revolver in your handbag."

"Oh." Mrs. Wembler's forehead furrowed, as if in puzzlement, but her eyes began to glint. "What about the gun, my dear?"

"Give it to me."

"What do you plan to do?"

"Stop Ungas of course."

Mrs. Wembler opened her military handbag. "He should be killed my dear."

"I'm simply going to scare him witless."

"With the gun?"

"Yes, rats scare easily."

Mrs. Wembler fetched out the revolver. "The law would forgive anyone, my dear, who killed that horrid man. It would not be murder. Yes, it would be best that you kill him."

"The gun," Kate said.

The gun was cold and hard in Kate's hands. She asked: "Is it loaded?"

"Yes, and perfectly safe. That's because the safety is on so that the gun cannot be fired."

"Six cartridges?"

"One, my dear, will kill that man."

Kate brushed the suggestion aside. "Mrs. Wembler, have you actually handled guns before?"

"My father taught me."

"Why don't you kill Ray Ungas?"

"Because I wouldn't harm a fly, my dear."

"Now, I plan to scare Ray Ungas, but I know nothing about firearms. I want you to instruct me, how to fire the gun, and so on. Ummm, it's not a very big gun. What caliber?"

"A twenty-two."

Kate rose. "Come," she ordered.

"Where?"

"We're going into the woods where you will show me how to handle this gun professionally. Ray Ungas is stronger than I and I must go alone to him. The gun must make me the stronger and there must be no botching of the job."

"You darling!" Mrs. Wembler said, beaming. "I could kiss you, my dear!"

Kate said tartly, "Don't", and left the room.

For three days, she and Mrs. Wembler spent several hours in the woods far from the farmhouse. Kate learned how to handle the twenty-two revolver. Mrs. Wembler taught Kate how to grip the butt correctly, thumb off the safety, finger the trigger, and fire. Kate actually fired the gun, but only sprayed bullets harmlessly in the woods. In sharp contrast to Kate's inefficiency, Mrs. Wembler proved to be an expert shot, hitting any tree she aimed at, up to thirty yards.

"You force the gun," Mrs. Wembler explained. "As the cartridge explodes, the gun bucks in the tight hand. To hit a target, you must anticipate the bucking and compensate so as to—"

"Never mind about my hitting the target," Kate interrupted impatiently. "I'm not planning to kill Ungas. If he should try to jump the gun, thinking that I only bluffed, I'd not miss him because he'd be close."

"Kill him, my dear, and everything will be lovely.

"For you or me?"

"For both of us! You face Ungas alone. He's a man, a black-mailer to boot. He attacks you because you are a woman. It would be easy to taunt him into attacking you. No, not that method. Kate, pretend you're not expert at handling the gun. Act as if it were the first time you ever had a gun in hand. He will realize your weakness and attack you confidently. Then, all you have to do is—"

"No," Kate said. "A rat scares easily. He'll know I'm good with the gun and the threat will stick."

Kate dropped the gun in her handbag. Casually, she opened the bag, plucked out the gun, wheeled on Mrs. Wembler, and leveled the weapon.

"Was that convincing?" she asked.

"Yes, until you leveled the gun. Don't push the gun forward so far, that's amateurish. Handle it more loosely, as if it were an extension of your hand. Bend the elbow."

"Like this?"

"Much better. Try the full movement, Kate."

Several times, Kate drew the gun from the handbag. When she thumbed off the safety, it clicked softly, a deadly sound in the silence of the woods.

"Better?" Kate asked.

"Yes, unless you plan to kill him."

"I don't. We'll go back to the house and I'll phone him."

"Will you meet him in New York?"

"Probably."

"Kate, I'm much older than you and more experienced. Don't feel that I'm trying to act superior, please."

"I won't."

Mrs. Wembler brooded for a moment. "I'm thinking of you, how you'll have the best advantage over this Ungas. Not in the city where his apartment will be strange to you, but familiar to him. Why not meet him here in Westchester? Not on my place, but nearby. Is he used to the city, Kate?"

"Yes."

"And is he at home in the country?"

"No."

"But you are, my dear. Here in the hills, in some quiet spot you know, set your trap to scare him. If he should jump you—that's a possibility—you must be prepared to shoot. No one will hear a shot in this loneliness."

The suggestion made sense to Kate, and she said so.

At the farmhouse, they saw Old Joe Cramer mowing the back lawn, but he acted as though he didn't know they were near and went on mowing unconcernedly.

Kate used the office phone at Mrs. Wembler's suggestion while the woman hovered near the door. When Ray Ungas answered guardedly, Kate asked him to come to Westchester late that afternoon. He demurred, and Kate said: "Darling, it's urgent." She doubted that anyone connected with Danny Dorman had yet contacted him, but she worded a question to find out. "Has the situation with you-know-who, the hot shot, changed lately, darling?"

"Very quiet. Oh—where's the woman, huh?"

"Mrs. Wembler drove to town. I'm alone here. Ray, are you worried?"

"Not me. We're gonna take that dame for plenty, see? Maybe I will drive out."

"Meet me at the woods lane, remember?"

"Well—"

"Ray."

"Yeah?"

"A full payment today, darling!"

Ungas chuckled. "Hey, you sound like my lovin' babe! I'll come."

"About six-thirty, okay?"

"Sure, sure."

Kate cradled the phone. "He's coming," Kate said.

"And I hope your plan works," Mrs. Wembler said warmly. "Oh, you mentioned some woods lane?"

"A mile down the road."

"And he's really coming!" Mrs. Wembler smiled. "Chill him so thoroughly he'll never again set foot in Westchester! Umm, which woods lane?"

"Near the parkway."

"My dear, as you draw the gun, remember not to thumb off the safety. If he tries to call your bluff, thumb the safety off. Don't fire at him, but one shot, even a wild shot, will bring him to his senses. Aren't there several woods lanes near the parkway?"

"This one is the first on the right off the parkway."

"I hope he runs like a scared rabbit!" Mrs. Wembler bubbled excitedly. "Really, I never thought to shoot him. Hitting a tree with a bullet is one thing, but to kill a man—" She shivered. "How that man scares me! At six-thirty, darling?"

"Yes," Kate answered, thinking ahead.

"No one with him, of course?"

"No one."

Immersed in thoughts of the prospective meeting, Kate passed Mrs. Wembler and went up to her bedroom.

Once inside, she leaned against the door and thought back. Unmasking Danny Dorman had numbed her for hours, but she was young and the shock had not been too profound. After all, she had consoled herself, only a silly girl would go romantic over someone who sang on television, and I'm a woman.

She had not worried about the recording which had been made of her conversation with Danny, knowing that she had been innocent and merely a dupe in Ray Ungas' blackmail plans. Taking Danny's money had been wrong, but she could return that in a day or so as she wanted no part of it. The events at Danny's place had convinced her that Danny and everyone connected with him had been so scared of possible scandal that they could not block Ungas and his scheme. Which had left the matter of handling Ungas strictly up to her. And she wanted the blackmail stopped.

At the vanity, she picked up a familiar book, "Stars To Steer By," and the book opened to page 61. Pressed between the pages was the forgotten daffodil, *Magnificence,* which she had picked before leaving home on North Street so long ago.

In a measure, this dead flower was very much like her dreams. No more Danny Dorman. No more nothing. Her mind seemed empty and her heart a cold cave.

Idly she thumbed the pages and turned to a poem which she had always liked.

"Afoot and light-hearted I take to the open road,
Healthy, free, the world before me,
The long brown path before me leading wherever I choose."

Beautiful lines, she thought moodily, sadness overwhelming her. You took to the open road, with Ray Ungas. Then, you were sick. Now, you're healthy, but not free. The long brown path is before you and it's your choice. It leads to the woods lane off the parkway.

She had been lost in her reading for several hours when a sudden knock recalled her to reality. Mrs. Wembler opened the door and peeked in. Her familiarity irritated Kate for a reason she could not fathom.

"What is it?"

"Almost six o'clock, my dear."

"Thank you."

"I will drive you to the rendezvous, my dear."

"It's better that I walk."

Mrs. Wembler worried: "I shall wait here anxiously until you return safely, my dear. And do be careful! You're so brave, so very brave! Much braver than I!"

The door closed and Kate laid the book aside.

Could she go through with this?

Could she stand up to him?

All that had happened in the few weeks since North Street, but so like the space of years!

At the vanity, Kate opened a drawer and drew out the bottle of brandy which Gloria Marden had given her. "It may help you," Gloria had suggested, "on some dark day." Kate poured a glass part-full. She sipped the brandy and sensed the warmth in her stomach. She sipped more deeply, feeling warmth and strength race up her spine. When she had drained the glass, the brandy had restored her courage.

I can handle Ungas, I can handle anyone! she thought as she dressed in a dark sweater and dark skirt. Off with stockings and heels, on with socks and sandals. And the handbag.

The long black road led toward the parkway, and she walked demurely, like any woman who loved the country, out for a stroll.

Just a meeting. Scare him. Kill him.

No, not kill him.

As she neared the woods lane, the sun was setting. The way was lonely and quiet with only an occasional car. She entered the lane unseen, went in further than Ray had parked that first, odious time. She sat on a log and listened.

Time lazed past. Engine sound on the road. Sound of brakes. She tensed. The chrome nose of a Cadillac pushed along the lane and she waved to Ray Ungas.

He stopped the Cadillac, out of sight from the macadam road. Grinning, he hurried forward.

CHAPTER TWELVE

K ATE slipped from Ray's embrace, stepped back several paces. "Not yet, darling," she said.

"I can't wait!"

"Ray, business first, and it's important." Kate opened her handbag. "You spoiled my makeup, darling." She dipped a hand into the bag and fingers closed around the cold butt of the little revolver. "Ray, things have changed."

"Wembler's getting wise to our play, huh?"

"I went to Danny Dorman."

He stared. "What?"

"I went to Danny."

"What's the idea?" he growled nastily.

Kate brought out the revolver. Ray stepped back, his eyes bugging.

"I've waited a long time for this moment—darling." Not even Ray could miss the sarcasm in the last word. "When I first fell for you, I was a sap. When I ran off with you, I was a bigger sap." Kate leveled the gun, the muzzle centered on Ray's stomach. "Don't try to rush the gun."

"Look, you can't—"

"I can."

"You went to—to Danny." Ray wet his lips, shook his head as if doubting what he had heard. "To Danny! Why?"

"I'm no blackmailer."

"You took Danny's money, didn't you?"

"I was a sap."

Ray took a forward step. Kate leveled the twenty-two. Ray's face fell apart. It was quite cool in the woods, but his face perspired freely.

"At this distance," Kate said quietly, "I couldn't miss."

His fingers worked nervously.

"You're through," Kate warned coldly. "If you blackmail Danny any longer, I'll find you and put a bullet in your stupid brain. If you bother Mrs. Wembler, I'll shoot you."

His lips moved, but no words came out.

He's a scared rat, Kate thought.

"I was lonely on North Street. Sixteen years old, jailbait. You tempted me. I was innocent, but that didn't stop you. I was a fool to go to you, a bigger fool to let you touch me. Right on this lane, you raped me. I was sixteen years old, Ray." Kate's voice hardened. "I don't care about myself. Danny's safe from you because I'll deny I ever knew him and you won't dare produce that picture in a courtroom. I'm warning you—no more blackmail."

"Kid! Don't you wanna be rich?"

"Not your way."

"No minks, no Caddy?"

"Not even nylons."

"You took nylons once! Damn glad to get 'em, too!"

"I was a sap," Kate said bitterly.

"An' a sap is always a sap. You whored with me an' you liked it." He goaded her, inching one foot forward. "An' not very smart. You did it for practically nothin'. I said to myself, 'She's cheap, she'll do it for next to nothin'.' " Ray laughed as Kate's face darkened. "Yah, you're just a cheap—"

"Stop it!" Kate warned. "Call me that name again and I'll kill you!"

Ray wiped sweaty hands on the jacket. As if he realized he had angered her unnecessarily, he changed tactics.

"Don't be a sap," he wheedled. "Why did you go to Danny? And what did Danny say?"

She remembered what Danny had called her, the same vile name that Ray had used. They were two of a kind, alley rats. The important thing was that rats scared easily.

Ray said: "What did you tell Danny?"

"The truth."

"What's the truth, hum?"

"I told Danny I didn't know he was coming to your rooms that night. I told him it was a complete surprise, that I didn't realize why you had snapped the picture. I told Danny everything, that I wouldn't be any part to blackmail. He took it down on tape and he had two detectives there."

"I met those two saps." Ray laughed. "They tried to chill me, but it didn't work. They knew I had the upper hand. I had the pic where they couldn't grab it. They know I'll shout my head off if they move so they don't move. Danny's scared. He don't know from nothing, kid, and—"

"Don't call me kid!"

"Okay, okay!" Sweat had soaked the edges of the scarf around Ray's scrawny neck. "Danny's no good, Kate."

"So I found out."

"Plenty rich an' enough to spare for us!"

"I don't want his money."

"Okay, okay." Ray had edged imperceptibly closer. "Let's work it different. Let's go away. I got money. We can drive right off. Head for Florida. Palm trees, Kate. Sunshine all day and stars out by the billions at night. We sit by the ocean an' listen to the waves an' we—"

"I hate you!"

"Kate! I was good to you. Didn't I take you away from those nutsy parents? Didn't I take care of you? Didn't I bring you to a nice place? That's good old Ray!"

"Yes, old Ray."

"Okay, so I'm older than you. What about California, huh, The Caddy's gassed up an' we can head there. I don't like Manhattan." He was aware of the gun, less steady in her hand. "Ummm, Hollywood. You got beauty. You got talent. Klieg lights, Kate. Movie stars. You rise to the top, see?"

You do have talent, Kate thought. Gloria Marden said you had lots and lots of talent. You worked and exercised, you're slimmer and harder. It takes nerve to face a camera. But not for Ray Ungas. Not with Ray Ungas. For Kate Flick, yes. Just chill the rat and—

He came at her in a sudden, agile rush. "You bitch!"

She had thought him cowed, a cornered rat ready to run. She tried to thumb the safety on the revolver as Mrs. Wembler had taught her. Ray's left hand shot out and grabbed her gun wrist. His shoulder slammed against her breasts, hurting her cruelly. She staggered backward under the impact. His right arm circled her waist, pressing her against him, and she knew that desperation nerved him.

For a moment, they fought silently. Ray held Kate's gun hand away from him and his arm tightened. His weight forced Kate back a step. She tripped, fell backward and dragged him down. He had not released her right arm. Her weight and his weight combined pinned the right arm fast. His left hand immobilized the gun.

He growled deep in his throat, an animalistic sound. His sweaty face worked against Kate's face as they struggled.

He'll kill me, Kate thought wildly. God, I must use the gun.

His weight held her flat on the ground. He snarled, "You stupid sap," and his fingers dug into her wrist trying to make her drop the gun.

When he tried to withdraw the right arm from under her body, Kate twisted to the left and pressed her body hard against the inside of his elbow. Her left hand was free. She sniffed the heavy scent of pomade on his short hair.

Kate reached over Ray's back and grabbed an ear with her free, left hand. She jerked. His chin lifted. His face screwed up with pain. She pulled harder, forcing his head back.

He panted: "Lie still!"

Never!

"Kate! Let's make-up!"

She kept pulling the ear, thinking: "I can't trust him. Must kill him."

Her grip was strong on his ear, her muscles backed by the steel put there by the constant exercising. How long could she hold out against him? For a moment longer, Kate held the upper hand. Gradually, his pressing weight began to tell on her muscles. If she could only get him off!

Suddenly, she released her grip on his ear, went slack under him. "Let's make up!" she gasped.

He grinned. "Like hell!" His left hand released her gun wrist and the hand grabbed her throat. "You asked for it!" Fingers began to tighten on her windpipe. Black spots danced before her eyes, but the gun hand was free. She pressed the muzzle against his ribs, squeezed hard on the trigger.

Crack!

The gun went off. As if he had been sledge-hammered, Ray Ungas relaxed. His fingers eased from Kate's throat. His face twisted in agony. His breath caught, wheezed slowly. A drop of blood spilled from his lips and hit Kate on the face. His head dropped inertly, thudding dully on her breasts. Kate dropped the gun, wriggled free. Ray rolled and landed on his back. She stood up shakily, staring at his limp body.

"Oh, you poor dear! You—you killed him!" Mrs. Wembler had appeared from out of nowhere.

"I did?" Kate shivered. "He—he tried—"

"I saw it!" Mrs. Wembler said. "Why did you kill him?"

"He was going to—to—"

She was numb, her mind dazed.

"It's all right," Mrs. Wembler soothed, patting Kate's shoulder. "We're both free of him, now."

Kate leaned against her. "He's—dead?"

"I'll check."

Mrs. Wembler released Kate. She knelt by Ungas. There was a hole in the jacket, under the right armpit. The cloth was soaked with blood. Mrs. Wembler unbuttoned the jacket, checked the wound. She bent lower and laid her ear to Ray's chest. "No heart beat," she said. She thumbed his eyes open, studied the pupils. There was blood on his lips. She said: "He's dead, Kate. Died almost instantly. He'll never bother us again."

Dead men don't bother you, Kate thought numbly.

"What can we do?" Kate moaned.

"Nothing, my dear."

Mrs. Wembler rebuttoned the jacket. She looked around, spotted the nickel-plated twenty-two. "I don't blame you for shooting him," she said, and dropped the gun into her military handbag. It landed with a clank and she latched the bag.

Mrs. Wembler asked briskly: "Did anyone see you enter the woods, darling?"

Kate shook her head.

"Just we three know about this meeting?"

"Yes."

Mrs. Wembler hurried to the Cadillac, opened the door.

He tried to kill me, Kate thought. His fingers choked me. I pressed the gun against his side and—

She stared at Mrs. Wembler. The woman stepped from the car. In her gloved, right hand she carried a gun.

"It must be *his* gun," she announced triumphantly. "I see an easy way out of this. I'm going to help you, my dear. You killed him and helped me. I will repay you. No one but the two of us will know you killed him."

I pressed the gun muzzle against his side, Kate thought, her mind still dazed. I pulled the trigger hard and—

"This is a forty-five automatic," Mrs. Wembler whispered. "The bullet is much bigger and far more powerful than the bullet from a twenty-two. Nobody need know you killed him, my dear."

Mrs. Wembler knelt by the body. The safety on the automatic snicked off. She cocked an ear towards the macadam road and listened. There was no sound from the road. Somewhere deeper in the woods, a bird caroled.

Ee—oo—leee, Ee—oo—lee! Clear and sweet, a wood thrush was singing.

Mrs. Wembler rested the muzzle in the jacket hole. There was a loud, somewhat muffled report. The body jerked as the heavy bullet went home. Blue-gray smoke curled from the jacket.

"Right into the hole made by the twenty-two," Mrs. Wembler said. "I'll wrap his fingers around the butt. They'll find him here. They won't know you killed him, my dear. They will see the big hole and probe for a single bullet, not knowing that it was your gun and your shot that killed him, my dear."

Kate swayed.

"No time to faint," Mrs. Wembler ordered. "Where's your handbag?"

It lay at Kate's feet. She picked it up.

"Did you carry a handkerchief, my dear?"

"No."

"Carried nothing which you might have dropped?"

"No."

"Kate, step into the woods."

Kate left the lane and leaned against a tree.

Like a dog on scent, Mrs. Wembler prowled the lane. Once, she knelt and studied the ground. With a gloved hand, she erased a footprint and raked leaves over the spot. She moved swiftly and silently, eyes darting everywhere. Satisfied at last that there was no trace here of someone else on the lane, she busied herself where Kate and Ray had struggled, and when she had finished it appeared that no one but Ray had been there.

"This way," Mrs. Wembler ordered, and led Kate into the woods.

Kate mumbled: "Why did you come here?"

"After you left, I worried. I knew he was a rat, stronger than you. That man and my darling, alone. I drove over and slipped through the woods to this spot."

"You saw—you heard it all?"

"Yes. Don't worry, darling."

Kate followed her blindly.

They reached a second lane in the deep woods and there stood the new station wagon. "No sound," Mrs. Wembler warned.

Kate opened the door, slid in. She eased the door shut quietly. Twilight deepened in the woods. Mrs. Wembler started the engine, leaned out the window, and listened. Headlights came along the nearby road and passed on, unaware that the station wagon stood in there.

Mrs. Wembler muttered, "All clear, my dear," and backed along the lane and on the road. She drove toward the parkway, did not flick on headlights until the station wagon was well past the lonely lane where Ray Ungas lay dead.

Kate tried to think.

He was cornered in the woods lane and knew it. He must have believed that I intended to kill him. When he gripped my throat, that was my chance and I took it. I thumbed off the safety and—

Her head ached. There was more pain in her breasts because he had tried to hurt her.

Mrs. Wembler, alert at the wheel, braked at the parkway, then swung north.

Again, Kate tried to think. Why did he jump me? He's a rat. Ha! Was a rat. Where did he find the nerve to jump the gun?

Because I *thought*—goose that I am.

I pressed the gun against his side and—

Each time Kate attempted to recall the events leading up to the gunshot, her memory would fail her just as she reached that fatal moment.

Kate forced herself to face the problem again, trying to relive the specific incidents which had led up to the death of Ray Ungas.

Death? No, murder!

Not murder, self-defense. He tried to kill me!

That revolver had a safety, she remembered. Did I remember to thumb off the safety? Was the safety already off and all I had to do was fire?

Fingers … throat … gun … black spots before my eyes. For God's sake think!

Did I thumb off the safety?

What is truth? Truth!

Truth is Ray Ungas dead in the woods.

Humming to herself, a smile on her face, Mrs. Wembler turned off the parkway to a narrow side road. Several minutes later, she reached the farmhouse by a circuitous route.

She said gayly, "Home safe and sound, my dear," and driveway gravel crunched under the tires.

CHAPTER THIRTEEN

I NSIDE the silent house, Mrs. Wembler helped Kate up the stairway and the girl was perfectly content to lean on the woman. Mrs. Wembler entered the bedroom.

"You sit right down on the bed and I'll undress you, my dear. And don't try to think. After you shot that horrid man, I did whatever thinking had to be done. You've no worries, no worries at all."

Kate sat down and closed her eyes listlessly. Sandals and socks were pulled from her feet.

"A nice hot bath will clear you of all this trouble," Mrs. Wembler said cheerfully. "After that, anything you wish to eat and drink. I'll fix a sedative, darling, and you will drop off to sleep like a baby."

Not like a baby, Kate thought.

"Very tired, my dear?"

"Numb."

"It was a shock to meet that awful man, but you cheer up and forget it." Mrs. Wembler tugged the bottom of the tight sweater from the constriction of the dark skirt. "Lift your arms, please."

Kate lifted and closed her eyes.

With a crackle of electricity, the sweater rose from her body and over her head.

"Good heavens!" Mrs. Wembler exclaimed. "You haven't a stitch of clothing under that sweater!"

Gloria taught me that, Kate remembered. Gloria said you're young and that in youth the breasts are firm enough without a bra. If I can remember what Gloria said, why can't I remember the details in the woods?

"Nothing under the sweater," Mrs. Wembler repeated. Doesn't the material itch your flesh?"

"A bit."

"I'll take care of the itching, darling."

Cool, capable hands rubbed Kate's back gently.

Aren't her hands rather personal? Kate wondered. If only I could sleep!

Sleep?

There would be no sleep tonight, of course.

The cool hands rubbed across Kate's breasts, massaging gently, pressuring a trifle around the nipples, but ridding flesh of any itching. A restlessness stirred strangely inside Kate. Inexplicably, she sensed a familiar arousing inside her body. Cool fingers continued to tease the tips, lingering overlong. There was an excitement Kate could not quell.

Mrs. Wembler murmured something throatily. Hair tickled Kate's chin, then the hair tickled her chest. She opened her eyes and saw Mrs. Wembler's lowered head.

Delicately, wet lips touched Kate's breast and Kate stirred uneasily.

Mrs. Wembler said, "Don't move, darling," and her hand found the flesh and pressed.

Kate gasped: "What are you doing?"

"Ssshh!"

There was avid insistence in Mrs. Wembler's movements. Kate pulled away.

"Please," Kate said.

Mrs. Wembler straightened, a smile on her face. "You're really very young and very inexperienced, my dear," she said quietly. "Lovely and desirable in anyone's eyes. So fresh, so young. Kate?"

Kate was uncomfortable. "Yes?"

"In the woods, I heard that horrid man saying such vile things about you. Kate, I don't wish to probe. Was he right? Did you give your body to him?"

Kate nodded dully.

"That's a risk, my dear. You're too young and precious ever to take a risk. Men aren't careful."

Kate waited, wondering what was in the woman's mind.

"Because they took risks with men—that's why the girls have to come here. They needed sex and forgot the risk, darling. No matter how young or how old we are, we all need the stimulation of sex. Sex is life, in a sense, something beautiful. There are better ways than men, my dear."

"I don't understand."

"And much safer ways, darling." Mrs. Wembler's voice was a purr, her face a red flush, and her eyes deep and fathomless wells. "Yes, much nicer ways than with horrid men, my dear. And never any risk, none at all."

Whatever was behind the woman's silly talk, Kate did not comprehend, nor care to comprehend. She'd had enough of sex and man's selfish desires. What she wanted more than anything else at the moment was a thorough soaking and a careful soaping in a tub of hot water.

Kate slid along the bed. She stood and stretched, forgetting that she was half-naked. She voiced a worry that was uppermost in her mind.

"No one will learn I killed him?"

"I was very careful on the lane, my dear. You saw me search for any telltale tracks and cover them. The woods lane now suggests that he went there alone to commit suicide."

"I hope you're right!"

"Of course, I'm right. Your sweater and skirt are stained with woods dirt. I'll wash them out tonight and iron them." Mrs. Wembler fingered the top of the dark skirt. "No one will ever learn that you killed him."

If she would only stop repeating that I killed him, Kate thought miserably. I just get him out of my mind and she mentions it again.

Mrs. Wembler unzipped the skirt and it dropped around Kate's bare feet. Her fingers a-tremble, the woman eased the slip from Kate's hips and it joined the skirt on the rug.

"Only one more garment between us, darling," Mrs. Wembler whispered, meaning the panties.

Kate said, "No."

"What?"

"I'll wear the panties."

Why, Kate thought, are her eyes so fevered? What in the world excites her so? In the woods, she was calm and controlled. Now?

Stepping around the staring woman, Kate hurried into the bathroom and closed the door. She began to run hot water into the tub and tried not to think.

Ray Ungas would not let her alone.

He choked me. He tried to kill me. I pressed the gun to his side and—

Her thoughts stopped short of some invisible barrier that would not let her mind through.

Why couldn't she think beyond a certain point? What blocked her mind?

If I don't stop thinking, I'll go mad. For heaven's sake, get into the bath.

She watched the water pool under the faucet. When the tub was half full, she shut off the water and fingered it. It was steaming hot.

As she stepped into the tub, she squealed as the heat stabbed her bare toes. Hands on either side of the tub, she sat down by inches, letting her flesh adjust to the heat.

She knotted her hair high. Gradually, she immersed until water lapped at her chin.

I pressed the gun to his side and—

"Stop it, you fool," she muttered.

With soap, she lathered her hands, washing them clean of the woods dirt. She covered her face with soap and rinsed off. When she opened her eyes, they smarted from the soap.

A hot bath was so utterly, utterly clean. If it could only wash clean her thoughts!

Carefully, she soaped her upper body, using a soapy brush to scrub her back. She lathered her breasts, noting that the hot water had turned them turgid—but she didn't mind that. The nipples were excited, nothing more. Hot water was not like cool fingers. There was excitement before the final sex act—and afterward. That was natural.

Why had Mrs. Wembler spoken so strangely?

We all need sex stimulation.

Always before, Mrs. Wembler had seemed above sex. Did she need stimulation from someone else? How old must a woman be before she lost the desire?

She's not sex, Kate thought, and grinned. She's all business, like a man at a cash register. Greed occupied her mind. Dollar signs cluttered her heart. Imagine, fifteen-hundred dollars for a baby! Imagine wanting only to sell babies, not keep them!

Kate rinsed off the soap. She scrubbed every inch of her body and began to feel better. At home on North Street, she had loved a soapy bath. Soap was clean. It freed you from anything dirty, like a man's moist hands.

Stop thinking about Ray Ungas!

The door opened and Mrs. Wembler peeked in.

"Finished, my darling?"

"Not quite."

"Hungry?"

"Not one bit."

"Why don't you try a broiled steak, darling? I bought some lovely T-bones in town this morning. It will only take a minute to fix one."

"No," Kate decided, and wished that the woman would go and not stare so.

"Coffee?"

"No."

"Hot tea?"

Kate didn't want any hot tea, but the offer suggested a way to get rid of Mrs. Wembler.

"Tea, please."

"Right away, darling."

The door closed.

Kate drained the hot water from the tub and turned on the cold. With a wash rag, she sponged off her body, closing the pores. She toweled vigorously until her skin glowed ruddily with health, peeped into the vacant hallway, then ran into the bedroom. She didn't wish to be alone naked with Mrs. Wembler, yet she hadn't minded, after the first time, being naked with Gloria. What subtle difference between the two women!

And there are no men about, only the old man. What about this old man—was he a threat to security?

He knew what went on here, or so he had said many times. Did he know about the twenty-two?

Did he know I took the twenty-two when I went to meet Ray Ungas?

Did he know Ray Ungas lay dead?

Tomorrow or the next day, someone would enter the woods lane and find the parked Cadillac. Other people, of course, must know about that lonely lane. When the body was discovered, the police would come, sirens shrieking. And reporters. Reporters always came when there was a body.

And what would the police think?

Suicide, Mrs. Wembler had said, arranging the details to make death seemed suicidal.

What would the reporters write?

Headlines, of course.

Through the newspapers, Danny Dorman would learn of Ray's death and disgusting Danny would be pleased at the news. No more worries for Danny. No more blackmail payments. He'd fire the lean man in the gray suit and the chunky man with the bold head.

Yes, Danny was safe, now.

The negative of the picture that had caused all the trouble was at a bank inside a safety deposit box. No one would ever view that negative. Possibly, the police, if they learned about the deposit box. Still, Danny would be safe from more trouble. No one could tell from the negative or a picture that the beautiful girl in Danny's arms was only sixteen, and jail-bait. The police would not bother Danny with the negative. Gloria Marden had said the police took a dim view of a blackmailer.

So, everything would turn out all right.

Except for old Joe Cramer.

The old man would learn the news that Ray Ungas was dead. He knew Ray. He would get suspicious, because he was a smart man.

What would old Joe think?

I saw the two of them go into the woods twice every day for three days, he would recall. I heard sounds of shooting from the woods. And they were together a lot. The night Ray Ungas died, the two of 'em went off, but not together. The girl walked the road toward the parkway, but the woman drove off in her new station wagon. Ray Ungas didn't kill himself, but those two know how he died.

If he suspects murder, Kate reassured herself, the old man won't turn me over to the police. He likes me. He's my friend and on my side. I've no worries about him.

The door opened, with no warning knock, and Mrs. Wembler entered, carrying a tray.

"Feel better, darling?" she asked, and set the tray on the night table.

"Yes."

In a bureau drawer, Kate found a nightgown and slipped it on. From the closet, she procured a light robe and wore that over the sheer gown.

Mrs. Wembler asked: "Isn't it too hot for the robe?"

"Actually, I'm cold," Kate explained. "I finished off with cold water and practically froze."

Mrs. Wembler poured hot water into a cup that contained a tea bag. The water steamed, the bag exuded color, and she stood eyeing the cup thoughtfully.

"You'll sleep well, my dear."

"I hope so."

"When you feel better tomorrow morning, I'll bring you breakfast and we'll have a long, heart-to-heart talk. We must get our stories straight, you see. If there's the slightest trouble when the police find the body, I will be your alibi, darling. I can swear to the fact that we went for a ride. North of here, which is in the opposite direction from where we actually were."

Mrs. Wembler removed the bag from the cup. "Sugar?"

"Two lumps, please."

"I happen to be a one-lump person myself, darling. I don't call it dieting. Milk?"

"No."

"Touch of lemon?"

"Just with the sugar, please."

Kate sipped the warm, fragrant drink. "Will this keep me awake?" she wondered.

"You'll sleep soundly, darling."

When Kate had drunk the last of the tea, Mrs. Wembler opened a rectangle of waxed paper and Kate saw it contained white crystals.

"Only a mild sedative," Mrs. Wembler said, "to make you sleep soundly and forget you killed him."

Damn her, Kate thought irritably, she won't let me forget that. I should be appreciative, but she's so upsetting.

Mrs. Wembler dissolved the crystals in a glass of water and Kate sipped. There was a slightly bitter taste to the concoction.

"All of it, darling. You do wish sleep?"

"Of course."

Kate sipped again, set the glass on the table.

Mrs. Wembler insisted: "All of it, darling."

"In a moment. Wait until the tea has settled."

Why didn't the woman leave her alone? Why didn't she go off about her business?

Kate folded the spread and laid it across the foot of the bed. She turned back the single, light blanket and the top sheet.

Slipping off the robe, she settled on the bed, conscious that Mrs. Wembler stared. Kate tucked the sheet around her waist and reached for the glass.

Mrs. Wembler said, "Drink all of it, darling," and picked up the tray.

"I want to sleep—and forget."

Mrs. Wembler added, "Drink all of it, darling," and walked to the door. "Good night, darling."

"Thank you very much," Kate said warmly, and reached for the glass.

Mrs. Wembler smiled and left.

Ugh! Kate thought, what an awful tasting drink. What had the woman put into the water?

She took another sip, made a face. The glass was still half full. "If I don't finish it," Kate muttered, "she'll feel insulted, I suppose."

Slipping from the bed, Kate carried the glass to the vanity and emptied the contents in a cup. Back in bed, she settled under the sheet and flicked off the single lamp.

Sleep?

Gloria Marden had taught Kate a few tricks for sleep. "No barbiturates," Gloria had advised. "They're habit forming. Try exercise if you're wakeful."

Kate inhaled slowly, then exhaled. She flexed her fingers, let them unflex in rhythm with her flexing toes. Inhale-flex. Exhale—unflex.

She yawned.

Sleep was near?

She yawned again and continued to exercise. Gradually, a delicious warmth crept through her body.

Soon, moonlight stole in over the window sill and advanced toward the bed. Kate Flick did not see the moon arrive. The sedative had been powerful.

She either dreamed or thought and she didn't care which it was, as she was relaxed.

Somebody kissed her lips. Somebody whispered.

Dear Danny, she thought, then remembered that Danny was no longer dear.

Restlessly, Kate stirred.

"Ssshhh," a voice soothed.

The bed seemed overly warm. Had she forgotten to take the blanket off? She tried to open her eyes, but her lids remained drugged and her body lax.

Under the sheet, Kate moved a hand and found her thigh.

Bare thigh?

But I wore a gown to bed.

Or did I?

Her hand moved up her body, reached her chest.

Bare chest and breasts, too?

I did wear a gown to bed!

She came awake in an instant.

"Lie still," a voice urged. There was someone else in the bed beside her, someone with wandering hands, someone with hot, moist lips. There was a pressing body, a warm body, nude as Kate's was, and there were fumblings, little gasps, urgent hands at her breasts, trying to arouse her to ecstasy, pressuring and whispering and—

Kate screamed.

The sound of her voice echoed in the room and rushed out the open windows. She started to scream again.

A warm body pressed against her. Strong fingers closed over her mouth stifling another outburst.

"Darling!" Mrs. Wembler whispered urgently. "Don't be foolish and scream again! You're having a nightmare!"

Kate struggled, intent upon freeing her mouth.

"Darling, with men there is always a dangerous risk. With me, there is no risk. You're safe with me, darling. I saved you today, remember? Lie still while I stroke you. Lie still and await the touch of my love. Lie still, my love."

Gloria Marden had warned Kate: "Don't let her see you in the nude, ever. She isn't married, never was married. Kate, she's a queen."

Queen?

Mrs. Wembler's hand on Kate's mouth was warm and clammy, as Ray Ungas' hand had been whenever he had touched her. She sensed the wild, roused passion of this older woman, the moist stickiness of a probing hand, and felt instant revulsion against this kind of passion.

But she also felt something else.

A stimulation, a titillation, far beyond anything she had ever experienced before. An irresistible lassitude stole over her. Her bones seemed to be turning to water. She lay back in the bed with a sigh, and accepted the caressing hands, the seeking mouth. A few moments passed, and Kate sprang up again. Her body seemed on fire. "Please," she whispered. "Please!"

Mrs. Wembler chuckled triumphantly, disposed herself intimately next to Kate's pink nakedness. Together, the two women sought and found a wild, blind delight, an intense and ecstatic fulfillment that left both gasping with pleasure—a pleasure which, in Kate's case, was not only guilty, but qualified by disgust and hatred.

Thrilled to the core by the joys to be drawn from this delicious girl, Mrs. Wembler quickly returned to the attack. But now Kate had possession of herself, and her passion had been spent enough not to be easily aroused again. She threatened, "That's enough! Stop. Stop, or I'll scream. I'll scream until—"

Mrs. Wembler's hands again came down over Kate's lips.

Kate opened her mouth wider, but not to scream. Her lips relaxed and the pressuring hand eased. Kate bit hard on Mrs. Wembler's palm and Mrs. Wembler squealed and drew back.

Instantly, Kate rolled free. She slid to the floor, reaching for the pull-chain on the night lamp nearby. Underfoot, some garment was flimsily soft.

"Come back!" Mrs. Wembler panted. "Come back, darling!"

Kate thought, the damned idiot, and found the pull-chain. Light winked on and Kate blinked. Underfoot, she saw the gown she had worn to bed.

She turned to Mrs. Wembler, her eyes blazing. Now, she knew what a queen was.

She hissed indignantly: "I'll take my risks with a man, not a woman. You—you queer."

Mrs. Wembler sat erect in bed, the sheet around her waist. She wore no clothes. Her face was flushed and intent, her breathing too rapid, and her breasts flabby.

"Darling, I saved you!" she whimpered. "Come back to me, darling. You killed him and I saved you. Please, turn off the light." Her face pleaded and her voice pleaded. "For God's sake, come back to me!"

Kate's brain was clear and her thinking calm. What motive had this dirty woman had for coming to the woods lane?

He tried to choke me. I pressed the gun against his side. Could she go on? The words came. The safety was not off, but on. When I pulled the trigger on the twenty-two, the gun couldn't possibly have fired.

"You," Kate said bitterly.

"What?"

"You killed Ray Ungas."

"I killed him? Darling, you are beside yourself. Why, I wouldn't harm a fly."

"I remember everything so clearly," Kate said. "When I pressed the twenty-two against his side, I had forgotten to thumb the safety off. I tried to fire the gun, but it didn't go off. All the while, you were close to us. You saw everything, you heard everything. You wanted Ungas dead. With Ungas dead, you were safe from blackmail. Yes, safe and rich. I didn't kill him and you know it. Over and over again, you kept saying I had killed him because you knew I was overwrought. You wanted me to believe I had killed him."

"I saw you kill him, darling."

Kate wheeled away from the woman's stare, not conscious that she stood naked. For a moment, she was not in this room, but back on the woods lane with Ray Ungas sprawled on top of her. She saw the action clearly, exactly as it had happened, and shock did not block her thinking.

"He grabbed my throat. He was going to strangle me," Kate said tonelessly. "He must have forgotten the gun because I pressed it against his side and pulled hard on the trigger. Yes, I meant to kill him. I thought I was alone and about to die from his hands. I know now. The twenty-two gun never went off."

Slowly, Kate turned to the bed. All color had fled from Mrs. Wembler's face.

Kate said carefully: "You taught me to handle a gun, remember? You taught me *too* well, Mrs. Wembler. Yes, a gun went off, but not the twenty-two. Although I pressed hard on the trigger, the gun never bucked in my hand."

"No, no! You killed him, I swear!"

Kate shook her head.

"You planned it that way, trailing me to the lane. You wanted to be sure Ray Ungas died, but you didn't want to take the blame." Kate's lips curled scornfully. "You killed, but you didn't have the backbone to take any share of the blame."

And, as she thought, Kate remembered more.

"When Ray Ungas was sprawled on me," she said, "his left hand gripped my right wrist because our positions were reversed. So, it had to be this way. I pressed the gun to his left side. The bullet which killed him entered his *right* side below the armpit. In his right side, Mrs. Wembler. You know and I know that I could not possibly have killed him and the police will know that, too."

"No, Kate," she argued. "You killed him."

"Why did you wear gloves?"

"I wore gloves?" Mrs. Wembler smiled. "Dear, you did not see or hear or reason correctly in the woods. Why would I wear gloves?"

"I don't know," Kate admitted, "but you did. It's all there for the police to piece together. The police will understand why you wore gloves."

"Kate!" Mrs. Wembler's face fell apart. "For God's sake, stop talking!"

"You killed him. You take the blame."

The woman still sat in bed, the sheet covering her legs. She ripped the sheet aside, swung from the bed, and reached for Kate. Kate stepped back. The woman came at her with a rush, eyes mad, arms opened, fingers clawing, lips spewing vile oaths. She closed in. Kate lifted one knee and rammed it against the woman's stomach. Mrs. Wembler swore.

She grabbed Kate. They wrestled around the room. The woman was heavier and older than Kate, and it was the woman's age which gave Kate the advantage.

Kate hung on grimly, tightening her arms around the woman's waist. A free hand clawed at Kate's face, fingernails raking deep. Kate released her grip. Placing both hands against the woman's chest, she pushed viciously. The woman tripped as she stumbled away. In falling, she fell backward. Her skull smacked the baseboard. She groaned once and went limp on the bedroom floor.

Maybe you killed her, Kate thought, staring at the woman's still face and slack lips.

At Kate's back, a man said: "Put on your robe."

Kate turned. Old Joe Cramer stood in the open doorway, a gnarled hand on the knob.

"Child," he repeated, "put on your robe."

Kate grabbed up the robe and slipped it on, knotting the sash loosely.

"I heard you scream," the old man explained. "Took me a while to get here. She tried for you in bed?"

"It was horrid!"

"Don't blame her, child. She can't help it. It's more illness than perversion."

"And we fought! I—I think she's dead!"

He walked past Kate and knelt by Mrs. Wembler. After a moment, he decided: "Not dead, unconscious."

"I'm glad!"

He rose and came to Kate.

"Why did you and she go into the woods for three days and fire her twenty-two gun again and again, Kate?"

"She was teaching me how to handle a gun."

"Why?"

"Because Ray Ungas threatened her and because he was blackmailing—I wanted to scare him off."

"With the gun?"

Kate nodded.

"When?"

"I made a date with him near the parkway. Joe, we fought and he tried to choke me to death."

"He choked you and you had a gun, Kate?"

"I was careless."

"And what happened, Kate?"

"Ungas is—dead."

"Who killed him, Kate?"

Kate explained it rapidly and clearly, the words running easily off her lips. About the safety being *on* on the twenty-two in her hand, the twenty-two not bucking as she pressed the trigger, but a gun going off, and the wound in Ray's right side, not the left, as it should have been if she had actually fired the twenty-two. Then, Mrs. Wembler there, wearing gloves, taking charge, impressing on Kate the fact that she had killed, then covering up tracks and finally firing a shot from Ray's heavy automatic into the first wound.

"She would kill him—but good," the old man agreed, and smacked his lips. "She's vicious. What will you do, Kate?"

"I—I don't know."

"She won't remain unconscious much longer. The police will find the body, never fear. The police ask questions, Kate. They backtrack. They'll come here. What will you do, Kate?"

She did not know.

"Kate," he said quietly, "in 1909, I was in my final year at medical school. A friend of mine got in trouble with a girl. They didn't love each other, had been experimenting together, and the girl was pregnant. They came to me. I was a brilliant student, so the professors claimed, but I did a foolish thing. I performed an operation, an abortion. I wasn't as brilliant as my professors had claimed. Kate, the girl died."

His voice was old and tired, but calm from the repetition of the story which must have occupied so much of his attention down the years.

"I suppose, Kate, I had a choice the night the girl died. I was young, a brilliant career ahead of me—if the death could be covered up. I made a choice, Kate, and I never regretted it. I went straight to the police and confessed. Of course, I went to jail. For six years. Kate, you have a choice tonight. You can run off if you wish. You can keep quiet. I don't know what is in your past and I do not care. You're young and decent and very beautiful. The newspapers will have a field day with you, but it's your choice."

It had been inevitable, she knew. Right from the first, she'd known it couldn't go on: mystery compounding mystery, ugly facts coming to light. She had played the game and lost. When you lost, you faced the music, just as Gloria Marden had faced the music—and had paid so dearly. Everyone had to pay up, like this old man had paid.

"Your mother?" Kate asked curiously.

"She died of a broken heart, I think."

"Your father?"

"After my day in court, I never saw him again."

Kate said quietly: "Phone the police."

"Good girl, Kate. Tell the police no more than you have to tell them. Don't hurt any more people than must be hurt. Of course, this place will exist no longer, but that was in the cards. Nylons, Kate."

"Nylons?"

"She's got to be tied fast until the police take over. I've work to do before they come."

"Work?"

"Two girls in the cabin. A check of her records. I don't want the police to backtrack on the girls or the babies. She's been careful with her records, but I don't want any names to be lying around for the police."

"What about you?"

"Don't worry."

"The police will hold you! You worked here! You know all about this—this hateful place!"

"Kate, I'm only the handyman." He smiled. "Just old Joe, handyman. I don't know from nothing."

They tied Mrs. Wembler with nylons, finally binding her face in such a manner that she could breath, but not scream. The old man went out to rouse the two girls in the cabins. Later, the station wagon left the house, returned in a half hour. The old man entered the kitchen. They drank coffee that Kate had brewed, then they went into Mrs. Wembler's office and checked her files. Here and there, they found names and addresses, little entries for money paid.

"The girls paid her seventy dollars a week for living here," the old man said, and grinned. "She was so crooked she even cheated Uncle Sam."

He burned the records that might lead back to the guests who had stayed here.

"Ready?" he asked Kate.

It had been a long time, she thought. Five weeks—no, only a trifle over four weeks, yet so much had happened. I'm older she thought. Yes, seventeen! Still jail-bait. Will that make a difference with the police? No need to mention Danny Dorman. Ray Ungas, yes. He blackmailed Mrs. Wembler, seduced me, and raped me when I was sixteen years old. Would that make a difference with the police? The law could not punish Ray Ungas, now. The law could punish Mrs. Wembler and the newspapers would have a field day and—

The old man asked: "Ready, Kate?"

"Yes," she said bravely.

He lifted the telephone receiver, dialed, waited. Then: "Get me the State Police, please." His voice was gentle and sure.

Kate Flick sat down to wait.

THE END

www.ingramcontent.com/pod-product-compliance
Lightning Source LLC
Chambersburg PA
CBHW052008240626
47153CB00008B/2786